BY NOW, the romantic suspense novel is firmly fixed in the hearts of millions of readers who savor that choice blending of mystery, adventure, romance, and exotic climates.

For all of them, and others yet to discover the pleasures of this genre, we are proud to offer a brilliant and beguiling newcomer to the field—Anne Stevenson, who makes her debut in this superb tale of foreign intrigue.

A
RELATIVE
STRANGER

Anne Stevenson

A FAWCETT CREST BOOK
Fawcett Publications, Inc., Greenwich, Conn.

For R. W. A.

A RELATIVE STRANGER

A Fawcett Crest Book reprinted by arrangement with
G. P. Putnam's Sons.

Library of Congress Catalog Card Number: 71-105592

Portions of this book have been published previously in
Good Housekeeping Magazine.

Selection of the Literary Guild, October 1970

Published by Fawcett World Library
67 West 44th Street, New York, N.Y. 10036
Printed in the United States of America
April 1971

For R. W. A.

Chapter 1

~~~~~~

When Julie was still a child, her family had spent several summers in a rented cottage in the Wye Valley. For the fishing, she supposed. Yes, it must have been for the fishing. Her grandfather had been alive then, and she could remember that he and her father had been away from the house very early in the mornings, leaving her and her mother alone. Sometimes they must have gone down to the river to join them. She had a memory of walking along the riverbank, holding her mother's hand. She had been wearing a white frock. It must have been new. She must have been proud of it and thought it pretty.

The cottage had been white, too; she was sure of that. The floors were stone, and there were flowered curtains at her bedroom window which looked out over a patch of orchard with untended plum trees growing crookedly in it. If you climbed one of those trees, the bark rough and dry, scratching your legs, you could wedge yourself high up between two branches and look down the steep green hillside to the river at the bottom, a hillside thick and green and impenetrable and concealing as a jungle, where only an occasional trail of smoke from a chimney or a flicker of washing on a line betrayed the presence of other houses.

Strangely, she only remembered Richard being there the last summer. She was nine and he was nineteen and had been at the university for a year. She remembered him — and the flies. There had been a spell of very warm, very humid weather, and they had been tormented by flies wherever they walked. She had been lonely, and aware for the first time that she was lonely. To have a brother made no difference when he was already a man to her child, an adult like her parents. She had been to all intents and purposes an only child. She had sat for hours in the plum tree, gazing down at the river, thinking of nothing, or had hung about the kitchen, stuffing herself with biscuits, getting under her mother's feet, until, banished outside again, she would start running violently, aimlessly, full of a sudden burst of energy that made her want to tear up and down the lanes, and with no one to expend it on but Richard.

He had been put in charge of her one day and had taken her for a long walk. The flies had swarmed about them, and Richard had smoked a pipe, puffing great clouds of smoke around them to drive the flies away and making her walk right up to the top of the hill to try to get away from them. They had come to a village and gone into a Norman church to cool off. She had been wearing shorts and sandals. She could remember the feel of the wooden pew against her thin bare thighs as she sat waiting for Richard to be ready to leave. A man had come in, the verger or some kind of official, and Richard had talked to him about the church, and she had fallen into a daydream in which the massive round pillars of the nave, the soft murmur of the men's voices, the smell of old dust, the oppressive heat that waited, crouched like an animal, for them at the door, were all mingled in her mind into a feeling of drowsy contentment—a moment that had been, that remained, secure, protected, peaceful.

She had not realized until the letter came that that was her strongest recollection of her brother.

The letter arrived in April, on a Monday, by the midday post. Julie was out when it came, taking a finished illustration to Michael Brent's office. Michael Brent was the art editor of the Lockwood Publishing Company, and he was encouraging Julie. He encouraged her by being as particular in his judgment of her work as if she were, as her sister-in-law, Dorothy, would put it, doing real painting. She had worked all Sunday to meet the deadline he had given her, and she had awakened with the carefree sense of relief of a job done, finished, ready, never mind whether it was good or not.

She sat waiting for his decision in the old-fashioned paneled office in the Edwardian block the company rented off the Strand, a building near enough to Fleet Street to be called Fleet Street by those employees who liked their work to be endowed with the racy aura of daily journalism, and far enough away, gloomy enough, echoing and spacious enough to please those who preferred an atmosphere of literary solidity. It had a tiled entrance hall with art nouveau vines curling and convoluting around the light switches and a single lift with openwork double iron gates which had to be opened and closed by hand for every journey and which jammed on an average once every six weeks. The sign which read ENQUIRIES was too small, and the door to the reception room was equally shut against the drafts whistling up from the river at the bottom of the street, with the result that visitors were frequently to be found wandering the corridors mouthing the names of the people or the departments with whom they had business and opening and shutting doors wildly on an increasing note of despair. All were eventually rescued by one of the charming and soft-spoken secretaries who saw them safely to their destinations, warning them on the way to be careful of the lift.

· The whole small company was a blend of deliberately cultivated amateurism and ruthless professional acumen, which reflected accurately enough, Michael Brent thought, the three Lockwood brothers who ran it. Michael intended one day to become a director. In the meantime, he enjoyed his work.

He was a slight thin man with amused brown eyes and a nose which belonged to a figure of more heroic stature. He had known Julie for more than a year and professed himself enraptured by her legs.

"Not bad," he remarked at last, tilting his head in consideration of her work. "Not bad at all. They don't look quite so much like pre-Raphaelite consumptives. That's quite a nice hand and arm you've got there. Hey, Anne—" He pulled his secretary around by the skirt as she passed his desk. "What do you think?"

Anne Latham was a small plump brunette of twenty-two, married six months, and extremely conscious of it. Her normal brisk efficiency already carried overtones of her new status. She dealt with Michael's disorganization nowadays with something of the resigned patience of a mother tidying up after a child.

She glanced at the illustration, three figures set against a background of summer trees, which Julie had propped up against the bookcase, and said immediately: "The girl's dress should be red, Mr. Brent."

"Yellow worked better," Julie said.

"We must allow our artists their inspiration! I think it's quite good. Very hot. It looks hot, Anne, you will admit."

"It looks sunny, Mr. Brent."

"There you are. A triumph. It looks sunny." He swung his chair around. "OK, Julie."

"It's all right? You don't want anything altered?"

"It's all right."

"Well, that's marvelous." She smiled happily at them. "Oh, damn." As she bent to refasten it, the large cardboard folder she used to carry her work in collapsed.

"Why don't you buy yourself a decent case with all the fat checks we're paying you?" Michael said.

"What? And risk my integrity by looking like a commercial artist? Please, Mr. Brent!"

He laughed and jumped up out of his chair. "Come on, my infant genius, I'll buy you a lunch."

"Oh, Mike, I can't. I'm sorry. I'm tied up."

"With some lecherous engraver, no doubt. When are you going to marry me, Julie?"

She shook her head, smiling.

"Well, if you won't marry me, when are you going to sleep with me? This afternoon—I've no appointments this afternoon, have I, Anne?"

Anne raised her shoulders in an emphatic gesture, disclaiming all responsibility.

"I'm seeing my sister-in-law," Julie said.

"Oh. Dorothy." His manner changed. "Come on, I'll buy you a drink, anyway. You're probably going to need it."

Julie gathered up her handbag and the folder, quickly patched up by Anne with strips of Sellotape. Thanking her, Julie thought, as she so often did, how satisfying it must be to be the sort of person Anne was, the kind of woman Julie really respected: practical, competent, down-to-earth, with a marvelous simplicity in their lives. Julie longed for order, a regular pattern by which you could number off your achievements at the end of every day and go to sleep contented: so many beds made, letters written, meals cooked, curtains made, shirts washed, everything finished and docketed or, if not finished, transferred neatly to the next day's list. It was because she knew she would never, could never, live like that that she found the thought of it so attractive. The world was divided, she had long ago realized, into Anne's kind of people and her own, and it was no use trying to be what you were not. She liked Michael because she recognized so much of herself in him, the vagueness about things he considered irrelevant, the periods of concentration alternating with self-indulgence, the waste of time that you found out later when you began to work again had not been wasted. How many times had she discovered that her senses had been working when she had thought herself merely dreaming: observing, noting, collating reflections, light, the expression on a face, the twist of a hand in a sudden gesture, layers of color, tones, depths, eyes, a mouth laughing. The person inside her who made it impossible for her to do anything but use her eyes, her pen, her brush, no matter how poor the result, how small the achievement, that person was never idle.

Michael held the door open for her, and they walked down the two flights of stairs to the street, or rather ran, as Michael seemed constitutionally unable to move at a pace slower than a run. He was very rarely still. His energy would not allow him to be. He never used lifts. He found it quicker to leap up stairs two at a time. He was always surprised when agents or illustrators flatly refused to go leaping with him.

They came out the door of the building, turned toward the river, turned sharp left and left again, and were installed in the local pub within three minutes of leaving Michael's office. It was early yet, and they had the small bar to themselves. While Michael fetched two bitters, Julie fed sixpences into the fruit machine. She watched the tumblers spinning and tried to put aside the incipient feeling of depression that had begun to settle on her with the mention of Dorothy's name. A cherry clicked into the first position on the machine, and two useless tokens were deposited in the tray. She put them back in, one after the other, losing them both.

Julie had not seen her sister-in-law for more than six months. She knew she shouldn't avoid her the way she did; she knew that even if she found her as irritating as Richard had eventually done, that was no excuse. In the circumstances, oh, God, in the awful circumstances she could spare the woman an hour or so, couldn't she?

And yet the last time Dorothy had rung her, she had made an excuse quickly, without even thinking about it. It was her guilt about that which had made her agree, almost too eagerly this time, to see her today.

She said, as Michael joined her, "I didn't know you'd ever met Dorothy."

"As a matter of fact, I've only met her once, at the wedding."

"Were you there? Really? How strange. I don't remember you."

"Well, I don't remember you either, if that's any consolation to you. You must have been what—fourteen? That ages me all right."

Julie had discovered, when Richard's name came up once, that Michael had known him, quite well, at college. They had shared digs together their last term, and though they had lost close contact with each other afterward, they had gone on meeting for the occasional drink until about five years ago.

"I followed by remote control the slow dissolution of that marriage," Michael remarked dryly.

"What happened five years ago?"

"Nothing much. We just lost touch about that time. The way one does with people."

"Dorothy says he dropped all his friends about that time," Julie said. "She considers it another proof."

"She may be right."

Julie looked at him directly. "Do you believe it was all true?"

"Don't you?"

She shook her head. "I don't know. I'm a coward. I don't like to think about it, about him — trapped out there. You feel so helpless. Did you see the photograph? A few months ago. It was in the papers."

"Yes."

"I didn't believe it was him," Julie said. "I couldn't recognize him. I know Richard and I were never very close. I suppose I saw him only about once a year, if that. But to think they'd done that to him. In so short a time."

"I wouldn't call two years in a labor camp a short time," Michael said. He glaced at her face. "Have another. Something a bit stronger."

"I dont think I've time. I want to go home and dump my case first before I meet her. Thank you, Mike, I must go."

He smiled at her in a kind, almost fatherly manner, and she thought: *He understands what it's like. Two years, almost three. They think you get used to it. But you don't.*

"You'll let me have the next illustration in good time, won't you?" he said. "I'll get Anne to harass you."

Julie lived above a grocer's shop in a small street off Tottenham Court Road, an area "poised," Michael Brent had observed, "between the phallus of the GPO tower and the womb of the British Museum. A very suitable position for creative activity."

Julie had three rooms on the first floor, a bathroom to herself and a lavatory she shared during the day with the three women from the typing agency upstairs. They went home at five thirty, and the grocer and his wife left at six. Julie was alone in the house until eight thirty next morning. She never minded it. She never thought about it.

The shop had originally been the front room of the jerry-built nineteenth-century house, and its glass-paneled door opened into the small front hall. The street door was left open during the day, wedged back against the wall, to give access to the shop, and for this reason and to save the postman the trudge up the stairs, the post for the house was usually left with the grocer, Mr. Morfitt.

Julie stuck her head around the door and whistled. "Anything?" she said.

Mr. Morfitt looked up from his counter. "Your phone's been ringing," he said. "Want any bread?"

She went in. There were three people in the shop: Mr. Morfitt, who was briskly engaged in laying out bacon rashers in neat rows; his wife, equally busy behind the sandwich counter, slapping together squares of flaccid white bread covered with boiled egg or ham or cheese in the daily ritual of sandwich making; and a solitary customer, a man, leaning against the counter eating a sandwich and reading the first edition of the evening paper.

"Did I have a loaf on Saturday?" Julie asked.

Mr. Morfitt shook his head. "Friday. It'll be stale. Have a fresh one."

"All right." She looked down at the strips of bacon, delicate pale pink with creamy white fat. "That looks nice."

"Have half a pound," Mr. Morfitt said at once. He whipped the rashers onto the weighing machine with the speed of a conjuror performing sleight of hand. "Half a pound." He winked at her and added another couple of rashers. "Exactly."

Every few weeks or so Julie came down and paid by check for the food she bought from the Morfitts. She knew she really ought to keep a record, but she never seemed to have the right sort of implements — small lined notebooks and so on — to do so. And since the Morfitts never seemed to write anything down either, at least in her presence, she wondered how they reached the total. Since it was always about the same, month in, month out, she suspected that they repeated the amount, regardless of what she had actually had. And the fact that Mr. Morfitt was continually slipping her extras with the knowing smile of the conspirator made her fairly certain that she was regularly overcharged. Still, there couldn't be more than ten bob in it, and it wasn't worth worrying about.

Mrs. Morfitt put a large efficient hand on the tower of sandwiches she had created, pressed it down to half its original height, and firmly bisected it with one cut of her knife. She wiped her hands on a cloth and took some letters from under the counter.

"Here you are," she said. "Four today."

"Thank you, Mrs. Morfitt." Julie balanced her loaf and her package of bacon in the crook of her elbow and took the letters. Mr. Morfitt hurried to open the door for her.

"Can we have the stamp?' he said.

"Stamp?"

"For the boy. There's a foreign one."

"Is there? All right. I'll bring it down sometime."

She managed to get upstairs without dropping anything and leaned the folder against the wall while she searched for her key. The doors on either side of the landing had been nailed up and their handles removed, and communicating doors cut between the three rooms inside to make a self-contained flat. Julie unlocked the central door, which led into a minute hallway partitioned off the main room, and held it open with her foot while she placed the food on the small table inside, tossed the empty folder through the connecting doorway into the living room, and picked up the bottle of milk which had been left while she was out. She dropped the letters on the table and took the food into the kitchen. She put the bacon and milk into the fridge and also the butter from breakfast which she had forgotten to put away and which had a suspiciously oily look. She hoped it wasn't going off.

The clock on the mantelpiece said ten to one. She was supposed to meet Dorothy at Fortnum's at one. Dorothy would choose Fortnum's. She went back through the living room into the bedroom and changed her shoes for a slightly more elegant pair. Then she discovered the broken strap, which she had been meaning to have repaired for several weeks, and changed back. She brushed her hair straight, then on second thought piled it all on top of her head and pinned it there, squinting at her reflection in the mirror as she did so. It looked neater anyway. She always felt as if she had to array all her defenses before meeting Dorothy. The cause wasn't really Dorothy. It was the situation they lived with, that separately they could cope with but which, when they came together, for Julie at any rate, became overwhelming, a dark cloud overshadowing everything else. It was now two minutes to one. She hadn't taken her coat off since coming in. She renewed her lipstick, collected her handbag, and went out, slamming the door shut behind her. The letters were left unopened on the table.

On the strength of having had the illustration approved by Michael that morning, she took a taxi. Not that she had much option at that late stage. She arrived at Fortnum's at ten minutes past one. There was no sign of Dorothy. After five minutes, thinking she had made a mistake and Dorothy might be waiting inside, she entered the food department and wandered around, looking for her and absently concocting in her mind a meal made entirely from tinned or bottled delicacies: lobster bisque, pheasant in wine, asparagus, mangoes, peaches in brandy.

"There you are. I thought we were meeting outside." Dorothy seized her elbow in a gloved hand, looking cross and virtuous. "I've been waiting hours for you."

Julie did not contest this palpable lie. "How are you, Dorothy?"

Her sister-in-law was a blond woman in her mid-thirties. She had been prettier than she was. Julie remembered her at the wedding as a fluffy girl, all smiles and giggles, clinging to Richard's arm. She wore her hair cut very short now, and it did not suit her. Her face was thinner than the last time Julie had seen her.

"Let's go and eat," Dorothy said. "I can't stay long."

She hurried Julie into the restaurant. As soon as they

were seated, she took off her gloves and lit a cigarette. She did not offer Julie one. From the state of her fingers she was still chain-smoking.

"I saw an illustration of yours in a magazine the other week," she said. "And Charles pointed out a book jacket with your name on it. I suppose it was you."

"Yes, I did do a jacket," Julie said. "Last year."

"They pay well, don't they? You must be coining money. I wish I could find a way of making some easy money like that."

Julie sighed inwardly and read the menu. This was an old line of Dorothy's. Once Julie had made the mistake of trying to explain to Dorothy the hard work and insecurity involved in being a free-lance illustrator, especially a young, unknown, and untried illustrator. Before she had got to know Michael Brent, before the slow buildup of commissioned work began, she had often existed on one poached egg a day, including Sundays, and had been very glad to get a half day a week teaching to pay for it. After rent and materials, food had come a poor third.

But Dorothy's remark this time seemed more in the way of an automatic reaction triggered by the mere fact of seeing Julie than the start of an attack. She seemed jumpier than ever. She ordered a salad and waited impatiently for Julie to make up her mind. Giving in to the unspoken pressure, Julie, rather feebly she felt, ordered salad, too.

"Have you any news?" she asked.

Dorothy stubbed out her cigarette and immediately lit another. "No. When is there any news?" They were out of earshot of the nearest occupied table, but still she glanced quickly around as if afraid of being recognized. There had been a time when she was often recognized, when she, returning from a vain flight to see her husband, had found her photograph on the front page of every national paper.

"I wondered if you might be going to see someone about him this afternoon. If that's why you're in a hurry."

"I'm meeting Charles, if you must know," Dorothy said. "At two thirty."

"Oh, I see." They fell silent. The salad arrived. Julie gazed down at hers without interest. She felt deeply depressed. All the excitement of the morning had evaporated. The long misery of Richard's imprisonment colored everything. Even the salad, the green of lettuce and cucumber and cress enlivened by the soft reds of the tomatoes, reminded her of Richard. Love apples, he called them. Only falsely named.

"You don't approve of Charles, do you?" Dorothy said suddenly.

"It's none of my business, Dorothy. Why should I disapprove of him? After all you and Richard—"

"You never knew Richard very well," Dorothy interrupted. "I mean, not really know him. It wasn't all on one side, you know. I mean, obviously — " She lowered her voice. "Sometimes I hate him for what he's done to me. Oh, you can look at me like that, Julie, but you didn't have all those photographers waiting for you every time you stepped out of the house. Someone pouncing on you for a description of your innermost feelings every other minute. It was ironic. If they'd known the true story . . . " She broke off. "Why did he have to leave me in such a situation? I mean it was over, wasn't it? I mean if your husband walks out on you, the marriage is over, isn't it? Why couldn't he have waited to get caught until after we'd got a divorce instead of leaving me trapped like this?"

She pushed aside her plate, the food half eaten, and lit her third cigarette. When she spoke again, it was quietly, with a genuine note of despair.

"I don't know how long Charles is going to hang about waiting. He's very conventional, you know. He wants to get married. But what can I do? I'm not a monster. How can I divorce Richard now? I mean, how can I? Stuck in that godforsaken place. I mean, what would it do to him?"

"He wouldn't mind," Julie said. "He'd understand."

"But what would it do to Charles' career? If the papers got hold of it. Me divorcing Richard while he's out there. What would it make Charles look, let alone me? Anyway, I don't even know if it's possible. There isn't any answer. Oh" — she sighed impatiently — "if only they'd exchange him and be done with it."

Julie sat up. "Is there a chance he might be exchanged? Have they said so?"

Dorothy shrugged. "You know what they're like. They never tell you anything. But the last time I went to see them they did hint at it. I gathered we didn't have anyone the others wanted, or else the one they wanted was too important for us to let go. I don't remember. They make it seem so complicated."

"They wouldn't have said that much if there wasn't a real hope. There must be a chance. Oh, Dorothy, how wonderful!"

Dorothy looked at her across the table, her expression slightly startled, as if surprised to remember that Julie was in any way involved with Richard, or might be concerned about him. She said unexpectedly, "You must think me a first-class bitch only wanting to get him out of there so I can get rid of him for good, nice and tidily and legally."

"Don't be silly, Dorothy. I think you've behaved very well through all this."

"Do you?" She shrugged again. She stubbed out her cigarette and looked around for the waitress. "You don't want to wait for coffee, do you?"

Julie had met Charles once, a tall, thin, dried-up-looking man, who did not appear at first glance to possess the qualities of a demanding lover. He would probably make a devoted husband, much more suited to Dorothy than Richard had ever been.

On the pavement in Piccadilly, Dorothy burst out, quite oblivious this time of passersby. "If he intended to be a spy, he'd no business getting married."

"We don't know he was a spy," Julie said.

"Of course he was!" she snapped viciously. She hailed a taxi and climbed in. "They don't make mistakes. Of course he was!"

She drove off without offering Julie a lift.

Julie crossed the road and caught a bus back to Tottenham Court Road. Back in the flat, she made a cup of coffee, kicked off her shoes, and sat down on the sofa to read her letters. The post consisted of a final demand for payment of her electricity bill, a tax return from the inland revenue, a note from her agent enclosing a welcome check, which meant she could now pay the electricity bill, and a long thin letter from France.

Business or personal? Julie wondered. Unlikely to be business; it would be typed. Personal? She couldn't think of anyone she knew who was in France at the moment. The writing of her name and address was thin and spidery with a great many loops. The envelope was that particular kind of envelope only the French seem to make, very thin gray paper, lined, she saw as she opened it, with purple. There was nothing inside but a postcard. A picture postcard, in color. Julie sat looking at it with a creeping sense of alarm. It was a general photograph of a city square: buildings, traffic, people walking along the pavements. It might be any city in France for all Julie could recognize. She turned it over, and the writing on the back leaped out at her. She jerked back as if from something alive. Richard's writing. Richard's firm clear hand. He had addressed the postcard to her, and on the part left for the message he had written: "Interesting city, marvelous food, having successful business trip. See you. R."

She turned the card sideways and read the printed inscription. In three languages it informed her that this was a photograph of Lyons. It was in Lyons that Richard had disappeared two and a half years ago.

Somewhere in the bedroom there was a pack of cigarettes. She knew there must be some cigarettes left because she hardly ever smoked. She'd bought a new pack and opened it when someone came for a meal, and they hadn't smoked more than five between them, if that. Six, perhaps. She went into the bedroom and began searching. She found the pack at last in the pocket of a coat. She walked through the living room not looking at the postcard lying on the sofa and went into the kitchen. She took the matches off the shelf and lit a cigarette. She stood smoking and waiting for her breathing to settle. When she felt calmer, she stubbed out the cigarette and went back. She sat down again on the sofa and picked up the envelope. There was nothing on it but that thin curling writing. No return address, no maker's name on the envelope, nothing. The postmark was blurred, but she could make out most of the name of Lyons, part of the department, and the date. It had been posted five days ago. The postcard it had contained had no stamp, no postmark. It was not so simple. She could not think what it could mean. Thinking about it, studying it, she began to feel a knot of tension in her stomach at the frustration of not knowing, not understanding.

Two and a half years ago Richard had gone to Lyons on a business trip, one of many he undertook for his own import-export company every year all over Europe. The visit to Lyons had had something to do with textiles. So much Dorothy had told her. That was all Dorothy knew. By that time she and her husband had been living apart for a year. She knew where he was because he had written to her before he went, enclosing a check for the month's expenses.

He had never returned. Whether he had been kidnapped

or had gone east secretly of his own accord, nobody knew. There was apparently no official record of his leaving France, but there would not necessarily be a record in any case. The single known fact was that three months later he had turned up in a Communist prison accused of spying. At his trial he confessed his guilt and asked for the mercy of the court. He was sentenced to twelve years in a labor camp.

The British authorities had played it all very cool. They had neither confirmed nor denied that Richard had had anything to do with them. Dorothy had continued to receive her monthly check, sent to her by Richard's company. As she had said to Julie, "I don't know where it really comes from, and I've got more sense than to ask. It's money, that's all I care."

Julie had had no letter, no message, no sign of any kind from Richard during all that time. Until today. Until this card with its normal, affectionate, commonplace message drifting like a ghost into her life. She sat still, thinking about Richard, remembering that day in her childhood when he had taken her into the church and the sense she had had of his protectiveness toward her. What was this card? A message, an appeal, an extraordinary coincidence? And coming from France? She could not understand anything about it.

She got up, slipping her feet back in her shoes, picked up bag and coat, and went out. She walked down the road to a cinema, bought a ticket, and went in. The theater was half empty, the audience the usual mixed bag to be found in any small London cinema on a Monday afternoon: a few foreign visitors, one or two women who had come up for shopping and lunch and were rounding off their day before catching their trains back home, some students, an old-age pensioner or two dozing in the front seats. Julie sat in the middle of an empty row, automatically giving herself room to maneuver in case one of the lonely Romeos who try to come and rub their legs against the legs of women sitting alone should choose her for a target. The advertisements were on. A girl came around, yawning, with a tray of refreshments, and Julie bought an ice from her and sat eating it and neatly avoiding dropping the melting ice cream down her coat. She abandoned the wrapper on the floor, folded her arms, and sat through a gloomy, erotic feature from Scandinavia without reading a single subtitle.

When it was finished, she got up to go. As she walked up the aisle to the back of the cinema, she noticed a man sitting two rows behind her. The face seemed familiar. She wor-

ried about it all the way home, and it was not until she was
unlocking the front door of the house, shut now that it was
past six, gazing as she did so at Mr. Morfitt's ambitious display of cereal packages in the shop window, that it came to
her. The customer in the shop that morning, eating the
sandwich. She had noted his face without realizing it. A pale
complexion, traces of acne scars on his cheeks, thin nose,
thin lips, hair brushed straight back from a widow's peak.
She even remembered his tie. Pale blue. Rather pretty. He
was the man in the cinema. She was pleased to have solved
one puzzle at least.

Her telephone was ringing. She slammed the front door
shut and ran up the stairs. By the time she had got the door
of the flat open and flung herself across the room to the
phone, the caller had rung off. She was left with the dial
tone humming in her ear. Slowly she replaced the receiver.

Julie had found already from experience that there was
one solution to any personal anxiety and that was to work.
Richard's postcard lay where she had left it. She placed it
and its envelope on the mantelpiece and then proceeded
to try to forget it. She banished the riddle to another layer
of thought, to be mulled over, examined, probed by her sub-
conscious mind while she calmed herself with the solving of
other, more practical problems.

The chest of drawers on one side of the room, near the
easel, was her office. From the long drawer at the bottom
she got out some sheets of rough drawing paper and pinned
them to her drawing board. From another drawer she took
out the folder of notes she had made during conferences in
Michael's office at Lockwood's, and the photographs of the
episode, posed by models, that they had decided should be
illustrated. She pinned a photograph to one corner of the
drawing board and began to make sketches. It was a scene
involving movement. She drew with quick vigorous strokes,
searching for the shape and balance that would create the
impression she wanted. She worked sitting at the long
table in the window. As soon as she filled one sheet with
human figures, she tore it off and began on the next. After
an hour, she had evolved to her own satisfaction the general
structure of the illustration. She began to draw in more detail
the head of the main character, occasionally stopping to look
at herself in the mirror, holding the same position, to verify
the pull of the muscles.

After a while, she took out a cigarette and went into

the kitchen to light it. As she came back the telephone began to ring.

She stood looking at it for a full two seconds before she could bring herself to answer it. She could not say why she was afraid or what she expected. Silence? The quiet breathing of an anonymous listener, the click of a broken connection, the dial tone's rough singing in her ear? The unexplained, the unexpected, the unknown.

She picked up the receiver. "Hello?"

"Miss Davidge?" It was a deep, pleasant, perfectly normal voice. She almost thanked him for it. "Sixth time lucky. I've been ringing you on and off all day. May I come around and see you?"

The trained politeness of a nicely brought-up girl was a barrier, Julie thought, to the sort of things she wanted to say: "I've had a terrible shock. I'm suddenly very frightened. I don't know who you are. Go away." She said instead, calmly: "What is it about? Who are you?" Too calmly.

He said, "I'm around the corner. I'll be with you in five minutes." And then, just before he hung up: "I've had a postcard, Miss Davidge. From your brother."

Perhaps he said that to make sure she let him in. Julie's reaction to it was, oddly enough, relief. Someone else was involved, someone else could explain the inexplicable. She had not imagined it. For even with the postcard sitting on her mantelpiece, Julie knew that she had begun to doubt its existence. It was not possible, it could not have happened, therefore it had not. When she came back from the cinema, she had been quite prepared to find the postcard gone.

When the downstairs bell rang, she propped her own front door open and went down to the street door to let the stranger in.

"Stephen Archer," he said.

"How do you do? I'm Julie Davidge."

"Yes." He smiled. "I'm glad to meet you at last."

The first impression he gave her was one of calmness. He seemed to her to possess above all the quality of being able to deal with things, to cope. The kind of man it would be an excellent thing to be with if you were in a plane crash in the desert, for example. In no time at all, Julie could imagine the adequate water supply he would find, the dates for them to eat, the plane repaired with the twisted piece of wire and soaring to safety. She smiled at the image it evoked, and he responded as if she were smiling directly at him. She felt at once an immense confidence in him.

"You're wondering who I am," Stephen Archer said. "I hope I didn't upset you mentioning your brother so bluntly over the phone. I was staying in the same hotel in Lyons at the time he disappeared. We spent a couple of evenings together." And then, when she did not reply, "I met his wife once, at the beginning of the trouble. I don't suppose she mentioned me."

"No."

He glanced around the narrow hall, at the shop, at the staircase. He was wearing a fawn raincoat, with a dark suit, a white shirt, and a black knitted tie. Julie's second impression was that he looked extremely clean.

"Do you live upstairs?" he asked. "May I come up? I want to talk to you. Something rather odd is going on."

"Yes, I know," Julie said. "It's been happening to me, too."

She took him upstairs. He looked around the room, at the easel, the drawing board, the unframed pictures cluttering the white painted walls, the table crowded with pots of brushes, with paints, turps, unfinished sketches, the cupboard covered with torn-out photographs from magazines and newspapers of faces and scenes that had caught her interest. He looked at it all with attention but made no comment. She took his coat and asked him to sit down.

She thought he must be about thirty-five or -six. His hair was brown; his hands were well kept, with square-cut nails. His eyes, she saw as he turned to look at her, were dark gray. She realized from his expression that she must appear much younger than he expected, and without thinking, she said, "It's not that I'm well preserved. Richard is ten years older than I."

He looked slightly startled. "Are you always going to read my mind so easily?"

That "always" disturbed Julie. Spoken so casually, there was about it an unexpected implication of involvements, developments, futures.

Looking back on that first meeting, much, much later, she realized that it was that positiveness in him, that decisiveness, which had alarmed her. There was a dangerous element about him, dangerous because so obviously to him the battle had been fought and won before she had even brought herself to face any challenge. It was to seem to her that he had summed her up in that first minute, made his decision, and then put it out of his mind. There were no intermediary steps. It was that undercurrent of tension which made their first meeting so unreal in retrospect. She could never have imagined herself feeling with such intensity or behaving with such idiotic simplicity on so slight a knowledge of a man.

She said hurriedly, "You know, I'm probably being very foolish letting you in. I don't know anything about you. I don't know if you are who you say you are, or even" — she went on, getting hopelessly involved — "who you're supposed to be. I mean, if there's something funny going on, how do I know you're not part of it?"

He did not appear to think she was foolish. Without speaking, he took a wallet from an inside pocket and, after flicking through its contents, handed her a driving license. It had been issued to Stephen Archer who lived at an address in Cheshire. Had he come especially to London to see her then? She gave the license back to him.

"I accept that you are Stephen Archer," she said, and added bravely, "Whoever he is."

He had seen the card. He went to the mantelpiece, picked up the card, and turned it over. "So you got one, too."

"Yes. It came today."

"You had a message on yours, I see. Is it your brother's handwriting?"

"Yes, I'm sure of it."

"What about the envelope? Is this it? Do you know this handwriting?"

The firm, deft way he handled objects, like the card and envelope, and his quick, workmanlike questions began to make her really suspicious in fact, not about the kind of man he was, but about what he was doing here, about his reason for coming.

"How did you know where I lived?" she asked. "You're not some kind of policeman, are you?"

"No, I'm not. What made you think that?"

"Well." She leaned against the arm of the sofa and studied him. "You sound like one. And you look rather like one. Like the kind of men who came in see me when Richard was caught."

"I don't know whether to be insulted or flattered. What sort of men were those?"

"Quiet, efficient, well dressed. They asked a lot of questions and never answered any."

He smiled. It was an attractive smile which lightened his

whole face. She grew to notice that when he smiled, it was never automatic or polite or, with her at any rate, a mere social gesture, but always sprang from real amusement and was always reflected in his eyes. And when he gave her his attention as he did then, it was a complete attention. She felt nothing about her was missed, not a subtlety of expression, not a breath, not a sigh.

"I'm sorry," he said. "I've been waiting to talk to you all day, and I suppose I got impatient. I'm not a very patient man." He pulled a white painted kitchen chair from its place against the wall, swung it around, and planted it with great deliberation facing her. He sat down and took from an inner pocket a long thin envelope with a familiar curling writing on it, and from the envelope a colored picture postcard. He leaned forward and handed them both across to her.

The envelope was addressed to Mr. Stephen Archer at his address in Cheshire. It was of the same quality as the one she had received, with identical purple lining.

"The same man must have sent them," she said.

"Yes, it would seem so."

The picture on the postcard was another view of Lyons, and the postcard itself was addressed not to Stephen but to herself in London. The message section was blank.

"That's odd," she said. "I mean it being addressed to me."

"Yes." He took the card back. "That's what I thought. Did your brother often send you postcards when he was away?"

"Sometimes. Not often."

"Ever two cards from the same town?"

"No." She stared at him. "No, never. But Richard didn't send these."

"He must have bought them, though. That is, if you're sure it's his handwriting."

"Yes, I'm sure. At least, I think I am. It looks like his handwriting. It's silly, I know, but I find it frightening. To get a message like this, from the past."

"I think you're right to be frightened," he said disconcertingly. "There's a smell of something very funny about it all."

"Mr. Archer, are you a spy, too?"

"First a policeman, then a spy. No, Miss Davidge, I am not a spy. I am one of those referred to as simple upright businessmen. My business is textile machinery. I put on my passport that I am a textile machinery engineer, and no one yet, I'm happy to say, has suggested that that's a sinister cover for anything else. Though with incidents like your brother's arrest cropping up every now and again, it makes you wary of crossing too many frontiers too quickly."

"I still can't believe he was a spy," Julie said. "I know it must be true. Everyone appears to believe it. But I still can't quite take it in."

"I liked your brother," he said. "If there was any way I could help him I would. We spent only two evenings in each other's company, but you can get to know a man quite well in two evenings."

She found she wanted to know if he had been aware of her existence before the postcard came. "Did he tell you about his family?"

"Oh, yes." He gave a curious half smile. "We told each other all about our wives."

So he was married. *What did you expect?* she asked herself. *Of course he would be married. Of course.*

"What were you doing there?" she said. "At Lyons, I mean."

"I work for a firm in Manchester," he said. "I sell machinery, and when it's installed, I go along to see that it doesn't break down or fall to bits. If something goes wrong with it within a certain length of time, I go out and see what the trouble is. That is what I was doing in Lyons. I met your brother by chance in the bar of the hotel, and we got talking. He told me he'd seen me before, at some conference or other. We were both at a loose end, so we had dinner together."

"Do you think he spoke to you on purpose?" Julie suggested.

He shook his head. "I've no idea. I can't think why he should. He didn't ask me to do anything for him or pass on any message to anyone. The next night I was entertaining a French manufacturer, so I asked your brother along. We came back to the hotel together, said goodnight, and that's the last I saw of him. By morning he'd gone."

"And yet someone sent you that postcard," Julie said. "As if you were a close friend. Someone who knew or could find out your address. It's peculiar."

"Yes."

"When it all came out," Julie said, "I mean when Richard was caught, did the police ask you any questions? I was wondering how they traced you when it was such a casual acquaintanceship."

He tipped his chair back slightly. He seemed interested, amused, and yet there was no sense of his making fun of her. He seemed on the contrary, Julie thought with a small twist of pleasure, admiring.

"You're bright, aren't you?" he said. "I went to the English police when the story broke, but they didn't feel I knew anything of great importance. I talked to your brother's wife too, but I got the impression she was not very interested in my story either." He paused. "I should have expected you to be clever. Richard told me he had a brilliant young sister. He didn't tell me he had such a pretty one."

As if she could read his mind, she knew he had been about to say "beautiful" and had changed it as he spoke for fear she would think he was making too obvious a pass at her. It was an odd sensation to read his mind like that. *This is dangerous,* she thought. *This is very, very dangerous.*

She offered him coffee. She apologized for having nothing stronger to drink in the flat. He said he would love to have some coffee and followed her into the kitchen. There was physically a relaxed, lazy quality about him that would, she thought, at any other time, make him an easy companion. She could see why Richard had liked him. He leaned against the doorpost, hands casually in his pockets, watching while she made the coffee.

She went on worrying away at the problem of the postcards.

"It seems to me," she said, "that the only reason a card should be sent to you, who had no connection with Richard beyond these two meetings, would be if there was some sort of message on it. And even so, that would only make sense if it had reached you two odd years ago. It would have had some significance then, when all this business was happening. But now, when it's all been over for so long, when he's been in prison all this time — Oh, it's hopeless, isn't it?" She felt the same sick exasperation she had that afternoon when she had sat struggling to understand what it meant. "You need the police for things like this, analyses and detailed checks and messages to Interpol and all the rest of it, but I don't suppose the police would be the least bit interested. It happened too long ago. Case closed, that's what they'd say."

"Richard's employers might be interested," he said. "Perhaps I had better try and see someone official."

"Well, whether the envelopes are old or new," Julie said, "there's no message. The cards don't mean anything. And I expect when we learn the truth of how they got here, we'll find it's ridiculously simple."

"You're wrong," he said. "There was a message in my card. It sent me to you."

She did not answer. She did not know what to say. And he said no more, looking at her without speaking. She was aware, in that silence, of the intensification of the link between them, the complicity, the unspoken knowledge of each other that was so terrifying because she did not see at that moment how she was going to escape from it. The silence stretched out for a space of several heartbeats, and when the telephone rang, breaking it, it was as much relief as a shock.

She went over to the table on which the telephone stood and picked up the receiver. It was Dorothy. She listened to what Dorothy said, and then put the phone aside very carefully and sat down, equally carefully, on the sofa, legs straight, feet and knees together, Stephen noticed, in the endearing posture of a small girl at a tea party.

"What is it?" he said. "Is something wrong?"

She looked up at him, her eyes wide.

"That was my sister-in-law," she said. "Richard's wife. Richard's back in England. He's been exchanged."

Chapter 2

The restaurant was small and cluttered, with worn carpets and good food, one of those which progress to bad food and new carpets as they become known. So far it still belonged to the locals.

At this time of night it was half empty. Their table was littered with the remnants of the meal. When the waiter came to clear it away, Stephen asked him to bring another carafe of wine. He refilled Julie's glass.

"You look better," he remarked.

"I feel better." She felt soothed and slightly somnolent, like a cat in front of a fire. She held her hand out in front of her, fingers spread. "See? I've stopped trembling."

He put his hand over hers, holding it. "So you have." His hand was warm and dry, and its touch seemed very familiar.

"I think I'm slightly drunk," she said.

"No," he replied gravely. "No, you're not. It's the reaction. Aren't you glad now I made you come out?"

"Yes, I am," she said. "I'm very glad."

When she had picked up that phone and heard Dorothy

give her the incredible news, she had been too stunned to take in anything more than the bare fact that Richard was home. It was Stephen who made her ring Dorothy back and ask her all the questions she should have asked the first time. She got some negative answers. Dorothy had been informed officially about half an hour before she rang Julie. It had been a secret exchange, and they were hoping to keep it secret a little longer. He had already been in England a week before they had decided to tell his wife. They said he was fairly well but needed rest. He was staying in a flat, the address of which they had not given her, but they said they would let her know when she could see him. They had told her she could inform Richard's sister as long as she was reasonably discreet about it.

"Should you be telling me all this over the open phone then, Dorothy?" Julie said, suddenly worried.

"The only people tapping our phones will be them, and they know it all already." Dorothy sounded snappish rather than relieved. She was annoyed that she hadn't been told at once.

"When can we see him?" Julie asked.

"I've no idea. Of course, he probably won't want to see me at all. But he'll want to see you, I expect, Julie." The aggrieved note was back in her voice. "Perhaps you'll let me know how he is when you do, and what he wants me to do, if anything. If he wants me to go through any charade of happy reunion for the press."

Julie had recounted all this to Stephen in her flat. And she remembered saying, looking at the two postcards he had put down on the table, "Well, we don't need to worry about these anymore. Richard can solve the mystery himself when we see him."

Stephen had nodded, and almost absently, almost without her noticing, picked up the one he had brought with him, together with its envelope, and put it in his pocket.

"You need a drink," he said.

"There's nothing here."

"We'll go out."

"No, I can't." She looked around vaguely as if expecting someone, Richard perhaps, to materialize in the room. "I might be needed. They might ring me."

"I don't think anyone's going to telephone you tonight," Stephen said. "And no one's going to come here. Whereas I need a drink as much as you do, and what's more I'm ravenously hungry. I haven't eaten all day. So get your coat and stop dithering. I'm taking you out for a meal."

He had taken her to the pub on the corner and given her two stiff gins, which seemed at the time to have no effect at all, then marched her up the street, his arm linked in hers, and into a restaurant she had often passed but never entered.

"I don't know why I've never been in here," she remarked, sipping the last of her wine. She thought about it as if it were an important problem she should solve. He watched her, leaning back in his chair, and smiled when she nodded seriously to herself. "Yes, I do know. It's because I'm timid. I lack the spirit of the pioneer."

He laughed with genuine amusement, and she gazed at him over the rim of her glass.

"It's true," she said. "I am frightened of strange places. And of strange adventures. Believe me, Stephen." She held his gaze. She suddenly wanted him to understand her, to understand what had happened to her. I am afraid of you, she was saying. Of the way you know me and take charge of me. I'm afraid you won't let me go. Let me go, she was saying, before it's too late.

He smiled at her. He looked kind and thoughtful and quite resolute.

"There's no need to be afraid," he said.

She knew then that she was lost.

They had coffee and lingered over it. "I may boast that I know lots of places like this," Stephen said. "All over Europe. We commercial travelers pass on these tips to one another."

"Are you really a commercial traveler?" Julie said. "I thought they only existed in dirty stories."

"You ought to change the company you keep," Stephen said, "if the stories they tell you are as old as that."

It was impossible. Everything they said. This unspoken communication ran through everything. Who do you know? he was asking. Who do you love? Who must I get rid of? She began to feel exhausted. She almost wished that he would go. She had had too much to cope with in one day.

As if she had spoken aloud, he looked at his watch and said, "I must keep an eye on the time if I'm not going to miss my train."

"Your train?"

"Yes. I've got to get to Euston."

"You're going back tonight?" How foolish she must sound, repeating everything.

"I only came for the day, to see you." He paused. "I'm very glad about your brother."

"Dorothy said he was 'fairly well.' Only fairly well. I don't like the sound of that. Do you think they've exchanged him because he's ill?"

"No, I'm sure not. It'll be a political exchange."

"He must have been quite important for them to get him back."

"Don't be so cynical. They try and get everyone back."

"I wasn't being cynical," Julie said.

He clasped her hands between his. "Come with me to the station."

"Yes."

"No." He shook his head, changing his mind. "I must see you home."

"There's no need."

"I want to be sure you're safe. I can't leave you loose in London at this time of night."

"I'll be quite safe. I'll take a taxi home from the station if you like, then I can scream for the driver if anyone jumps out at me."

"Well, your brother is back now," he said enigmatically, "so I expect it's all right."

"You really thought there might be danger?" Julie asked. "You mean in connection with those cards."

He shrugged. "I didn't know what to think. Anyway, it's all over now." He looked at his watch again. "I must go. Come on."

They went out into a night street made mysterious by its emptiness. The air was damp, and the pavements gleamed as if they had that minute been sprayed by a water cart, but no rain had fallen. Outside every door of shop or office the dustbins stood, flanked by subsidiary piles of jumbled litter: extraordinary things you wouldn't expect to get thrown away, like lampshades and bookcases, shoes and hats, a carton of envelopes, an electric heater. And it was the same every night, Julie thought, as if the inhabitants were fighting an endless battle against some monstrous invasion of objects, winning each night some meager leeway for the day.

They came to the main road and began looking for a taxi. A bus came into view on its last journey of the night, and Julie suggested they get on it.

"No," Stephen said. "I want to be sure you've got a taxi to take you back. The one we get can wait for you."

When a cruising cab came by, they flagged it down and got into it. They sat in silence. He gripped her hand hard all the way to Euston.

As they walked into the wide, modern hall of the station, Julie noticed that they had reached the point in the cycle of the city when the day-people have vanished and the next shift of the population, the owners of the night, come out. Metallic echoes, footsteps, whispering voices—everything seemed magnified.

The cab driver had said when he dropped them he would wait for her by the side entrance.

"I hope I find my way to the right place," she said.

Stephen stopped. He was still holding her hand. "Come on." He turned.

"What are you doing?"

"I'm going to put you in the taxi and send you home."

"No." She smiled. "No, really, it's perfectly all right. I was joking. If I get lost I'll ask someone."

"Well, ask someone in uniform."

"Yes, sir."

"Someone in a railway uniform, not a licentious soldier."

"Or airman."

"Or airman." He sighed.

She felt like crying. "You mustn't miss your train. Your wife will worry."

He looked at her for a long moment without speaking and then began walking forward again very quickly, pulling her along. She had to double her steps to keep up.

"When I talked to your brother about my wife, two and a half years ago in Lyons," he said in a matter-of-fact voice, "I was in the middle of a divorce. My wife left me. She went off with another man." He made a sharp turn left. "This is the platform. And that, I presume, is the train." He looked up at the station clock. "Ten minutes to go. Very efficient of us."

They went through the gate and down the sloping ramp. All the other passengers seemed to have already boarded. Julie had the impression they were alone on the platform. He opened a door into the train corridor and climbed in. Then he stepped down again and came up to Julie and kissed her.

"I can't imagine anyone leaving you," she said.

"Neither could I," he said. "I was very surprised."

"Who did she go off with?"

"A museum curator."

"Good heavens."

"I suppose his virtue was that he stayed in his museum. If he wandered at all it was into the past. I was away from home a lot. She got bored."

"I'm very sorry. It was an awful thing to happen."

"It didn't matter. When she no longer wanted me," Stephen said, "I no longer wanted her."

"Was it as simple as that?" Julie said.

"No. But I made it be."

He would, she thought. *Yes, he would do that.*

"If you don't get on the train," she said, "it will go without you."

"That's what I'd like it to do."

She wanted to say, Stay, please stay, but she would not say it. She smiled at him. "Go on. Go home."

"I haven't got a home anymore."

"You won't melt me by sounding pathetic, Mr. Archer."

He climbed on board. "Good-bye, good-bye, my dear Miss Davidge."

She gave in. "When are you coming back?"

"I'll ring you tomorrow night. Go straight back home."

"I'll try to." The whistle blew. "Would you believe it. You're on time."

"Are you really crying?" he said. "Is it possible?"

"Of course I'm not. It's the light."

"Darling," he said, as the train drew out. At least, it sounded like "darling."

Julie went to sleep that night with a wholehearted plunge into oblivion that carried her too deep to remember her dreams. She awoke feeling marvelous, as if her lungs were full of sea air, and leaped out of bed, she who usually crawled, dressing gown tied around her, to make the tea.

She went downstairs to pick up the paper and met two of the girls from the typing agency coming in.

"Hullo!" She felt wonderfully sinful, still in her dressing gown at nine fifteen.

"Hullo, Miss Davidge, how are you?" They sidled past her, already exhausted by their journeys from the suburbs. As soon as they got upstairs, they would be putting the kettle on for the instant coffee, and in ten minutes they'd be rattling down to buy sticky buns from Mr. Morfitt and to borrow a look at his *Daily Mirror* over their coffee break.

The one in charge, a lady in her forties with tightly curled hair, never arrived till twenty-five to ten, and the typewriters never really got going till ten. It would be much more sensible, Julie often thought, if they all had an extra half hour in bed and started work at a civilized hour as she did, but she supposed the demands of the system wouldn't allow it.

She was having her own coffee break when Dorothy arrived.

"My goodness," Julie said, "you look very nineteen-forties."

Dorothy frowned, "What do you mean?"

"The fox, that curling fox!" She waved her brush at the fur stole Dorothy wore slung around her shoulders.

Dorothy plumped down in a chair. "Well, I didn't think it would take you like this, Julie. You're sometimes very childish."

"It's true, isn't it?" Julie said. "I didn't imagine it all. Richard really is back?"

"Yes." She took off her fur and draped it over the arm of the sofa. "I've seen him."

"Ah . . . " Julie sank down beside her. "How is he, Dorothy? What did he say?"

But she had to wait. Dorothy would not be done out of her preliminaries.

"After I'd talked to you the second time, Julie, I spoke to Charles, and he thought I should insist on seeing Richard, so I kept ringing that number, you know the one they gave me in case I was pestered by reporters and so on. I kept ringing until someone answered, and I simply said I had to see my husband. After all, I told them, he'd been in England a whole week before anyone thought to inform me, and to try to keep him from his family was really criminal. In the end, one of their young men came around, and this morning they fetched me in a car and took me to him."

"Where is he?" Julie asked.

"In a flat in Hampstead. Quite nice, near the heath."

"How is he?" Julie said again.

Dorothy took out a pack of cigarettes and lighted one for herself. She inhaled and let out a long stream of smoke. "I don't know," she said.

Julie felt the stirrings of an all-too-familiar impatience. "Dorothy, what do you mean you don't know? If you've seen Richard, you must know how he is."

Dorothy moved her head slowly from side to side. She seemed strangely unoffended.

"I'm not being stupid, Julie. I mean it. He looks awful, he didn't talk much, he didn't seem particularly pleased to see me." She shrugged. "Well, there's nothing unusual about that, at least, but he was all those things in a different way, if you can understand what I mean. A different way from the way he would have been before he left. I talked to the man who took me there about it, and he said it was only natural Richard should seem changed by what he'd been through. He said he'd be a great deal better when he'd had some rest and decent food. That's why I said I don't know. Considering all that's happened to him, I suppose he's all right. But I ought to warn you, he's not the same man who left here."

Julie felt chilled. "Did he say anything about his experiences?"

"Only that he was glad to be home." She glanced at Julie with a glimmer of humor. "He kept all my cigarettes. I had to buy some more on my way here. That was more like the old Richard."

"I wish I could see him. Can you give me his address?"

"I don't think I'm supposed to."

"Well, give me that number you ring."

"I tell you what I'll do. I'll ring them when I get home and tell them you're very anxious to see him. But it would be better to wait, Julie, until he's more himself. I'm sure it would."

"Dorothy, you're making me imagine the most terrible things—that he's in some doddering coma like that old man in the *Tale of Two Cities* who keeps thinking he's back in the Bastille."

"Oh, don't be so ridiculous. He's perfectly all right. He just looks different, that's all. I expect it's the teeth."

"What teeth?"

"His. He lost some in the prison camp and hasn't been to a dentist yet. It changes the shape of your mouth, you know."

"Dorothy—" In spite of her anxiety, Julie found she was laughing. "You make everything so confused and dramatic. Do you simply mean he's exhausted and ill and not recovered from the prison and he doesn't want to see anyone yet, not even his wife or sister?"

"I suppose you could put it like that."

"Well, I wish you had. You didn't talk about your divorce, did you?"

"No, of course not. There's plenty of time for that." She

got up. "Where do you spend a penny in this place? It's not in the flat, is it?"

"One landing down, door facing."

Julie collected the coffee cups and took them into the kitchen. Dorothy worried her. Not so much by what she had said about Richard as the way she had said it. Nobody, as Richard had once remarked, could call Dorothy hypersensitive, but she was obviously very disturbed by what she had seen. Something was wrong. He must be really ill. But wouldn't they have put him in a hospital?

"It's such a primitive arrangement," Dorothy remarked plaintively, coming back into the flat. "You ought to insist on the landlord building you a proper bathroom. I'm sure there must be something about it in the bylaws."

"If they touched a single brick, I think the whole house would collapse," Julie said. "It was run up in a hurry in eighteen hundred and something, and it's beginning to feel its age. It's due to come down in another ten years or so anyway, so I don't think they're going to bother with refinements now."

"Why do you stay here? Surely you can find somewhere nicer."

"It suits me," Julie said. "And it's cheap."

"Well, all I know"—pulling on her gloves—"I wouldn't want to be alone here at night. You haven't got rats, have you?"

Julie laughed. "Oh, Dorothy! Now go away. And don't forget your fur." She picked it up. "Was this for Richard's benefit or Charles'?"

Unexpectedly, Dorothy leaned forward and gave her a quick peck on the cheek. "Take care of yourself, Julie."

It wasn't at all the same Dorothy as usual.

Julie cooked herself bacon and eggs that evening so that she wouldn't be out when Stephen telephoned. She decided, since she found it impossible after Dorothy's visit to concentrate on anything serious, to do a lot of domestic jobs. She would do all her washing, sort out her clothes, put things out for cleaning and mending, get the flat in some sort of order for a change.

She started well by filling the sink with suds and washing everything she could lay hands on, including, by mistake, the nightdress she was using. She would have to sleep in her skin that night. She strung the dripping clothes on the bathroom line and then felt so exhausted she couldn't face anything else. By a major effort of will she took out a dress whose hem she knew needed resewing, found a needle and thread, and forced herself to sit still until she had finished it. She hung it up in the wardrobe, feeling virtuous, and swept everything else into a drawer. Enough was enough.

After such an expenditure of energy she had a great desire for something sweet. She had nothing in the cupboard that would do except for a large tin of apricots, which would have been too much to open for one. What she wanted was a small bar of chocolate. Attached to the outside wall of Mr. Morfitt's shop was a machine that dispensed chocolate for a sixpence. Julie happened to know it was filled on Tuesdays. And she had, she discovered, a sixpence. She propped the flat door open so that she would hear the phone and ran downstairs. She propped open the front door of the house also with the iron wedge used during the day and got her chocolate. She closed and bolted the front door again and set off up the stairs. She was halfway up the first flight when she heard a noise in the basement. She stopped, her hand on the bannister. The sound came again, not very loud, but as if someone were moving about down there. She went back a few steps and called, "Mr. Morfitt, is that you?"

She had never been in the basement, but she knew that there were two cellars there, one facing the front, one the back of the house, and that Mr. Morfitt used them for storage, tins, cartons, and so on. It was unusual for him to be working at night. She went down the rest of the stairs to the hall.

"Mr. Morfitt," she called again. "Are you down there?"

There is something unsettling about calling out to a person you are sure is there and getting no reply. The silence urges the imagination on to grotesque fancies. The sounds had stopped, but Julie knew something alive was in the basement. She could feel it listening. Would Mr. Morfitt behave like that? Could it be a burglar? Or perhaps it was a cat, trapped inside when a window shut. *You haven't got rats, have you?* Dorothy had asked.

"Hullo! Is anyone down there?" Her voice had lost its confidence. It sounded thin and uncertain.

She thought about it rationally for a moment. What would a burglar want in this house? There was nothing worth stealing. If it wasn't an intruder, then it must be Mr. Morfitt. He hadn't answered because he'd shut the door and hadn't heard her. And if it wasn't him, then it was a cat. If not a cat, then the wind, a broken window. It could even be rats. Why not? They would be attracted by food, wouldn't they? She would have to go down and see.

She took a reluctant step toward the half-open door that led to the shadowy depths of the basement and then heard, with the relief of a novice standing by an open plane door being told he needn't make the parachute jump after all, the telephone begin to ring in her flat.

She took the stairs two at a time and lifted the receiver at the fifth ring.

"It's Stephen Archer here," said the voice. "Is that you, Julie?"

She sat hugging the receiver close to her face, the mouthpiece touching her mouth. It was strange how quickly time had passed since they had met. It seemed much more than twenty-four hours since he had first stepped into this house, longer than a day that they had been apart.

He had to go to Germany the following day, he told her. He was flying.

"From London?"

"No, direct from here."

"Has some of your machinery fallen to bits?" she asked. He laughed. "Not quite."

"How long will you be gone?"

"About a week, perhaps less."

"Be careful," she said. "Don't get lost like Richard."

"Have you seen him?" he asked.

"No, not yet. Dorothy, his wife, has. She thinks he's ill."

"It wouldn't be surprising."

"No, I suppose not."

"What are you doing?" he asked. "What were you doing when I rang?"

She hesitated. "I'd had a fright. I thought there was someone in the basement."

"And was there?"

She didn't tell him she hadn't looked. Talking to another person, someone in the sensible world outside the house, particularly someone as calm and confident as Stephen, was all she had needed to make her fears dissolve. She had been like a child afraid of the dark, imagining terrors. Nothing frightening happened in this house; nothing ever had. It had a friendly atmosphere. Dorothy must have upset her more than she realized for her to start troubling about odd noises in an old house.

Besides, she could not let him go to Germany worrying about her.

"No," she said. "There was nobody there."

"Have you locked your front door?"

"Yes."

"Keep it locked till I get to London. I don't want you to get lost either."

She asked when he would be in London, and he said, "As soon as I get back from Germany."

When she put the phone down, Julie did not at once get up from her chair. While she was speaking to Stephen, she had felt calm and protected, even though he was many miles from her and could protect her against nothing. But now the link was broken and with it, if she was not careful, would vanish her new mood of reasoned common sense. When she realized she had not moved from the seat because she was absorbed in listening, she got up and walked steadily downstairs. She pushed wide open the door to the cellar, switched on the light, and went down the flight of steps. At the bottom was a corridor. The air was colder here and smelt of rotting plaster. Both cellar doors were closed and both locked. The corridor went beyond them to the back of the house, ending in a door which she presumed must open out into the sooty yard, tangled with the discarded ironmongery of past inhabitants, that you could see, if you wished to, from the lavatory window. This door was not only bolted and locked shut but nailed solidly into its frame as well. It looked as if it hadn't been opened for a hundred years. There was no sign of any disturbance.

She gave a small sigh of relief and went back up the stairs, closing the cellar door firmly behind her. There were two lights in the entrance hall of the house, one above the staircase and one near the front door. She went to switch off the one near the front door and paused. She remembered coming in from buying the bar of chocolate and shutting that front door. She had pushed home the bolts. She knew without a shadow of doubt that she had done so. But now the door was unbolted. Someone had left the house by that door while she was upstairs talking to Stephen. So it had not been rats in the cellar, after all.

All mysteries, Julie told herself at intervals during a wakeful night, have rational solutions. She clung to the word "rational." It was her new talisman. It had occurred to her that she did not know Stephen's address. She had seen it but couldn't remember it, and he had taken the envelope with it away with him. She had no way of getting in touch with him. At four o'clock she got up and made a cup of tea. She carried it into the bedroom and got back into bed, still wearing her dressing gown. From the bookcase beside the bed she took out a copy of *Emma,* a tried soother for restless nights, and read till five. She fell asleep with the book in her hand and woke again at seven when turning, she knocked the book to the floor. She lay looking at the light filtering through the curtains and decided to get up.

April in London is either exhilarating or depressing; there are no half measures to it. Today, she saw, was one of the lowering kind. From a sky stretched evenly over the rooftops like a canvas sheet a gray listless drizzle descended. Moisture slid down the window as if smeared by a dirty finger.

Julie ran a bath and poured into it the last drops of old Christmas presents. Strange mixtures of musk and flowers eddied up into the steam. As a last gesture of defiance, she washed her hair and ate a large and extravagant breakfast of two eggs, several rashers of bacon, two slices of toast smothered in butter and marmalade, with a head like a porcupine stuffed with curlers. By half past eight, when the Morfitts arrived to open up the shop, she was dressed, brushed, fed, made up, and ready to tackle anyone.

She was downstairs early enough to take the first post in. Mr. Morfitt was there in his shirtsleeves, both doors open, sweeping out the shop. Julie picked out her newspaper and the bundle of letters from the box, extracted the two addressed to her, neither of them of any interest, and took the rest into the grocer's. Mr. Morfitt leaned his broom against the counter and accepted the post from her, putting it on the shelf behind him.

"You're up early," he said.

"You were up late, weren't you?" she said.

"No, no." He smiled in a way that could be described as roguish reproval—almost—if it were not too early in the morning for even Mr. Morfitt to begin his false flirtation. "We're never late during the working week. Saturdays, yes, but weekdays, early to bed is essential, I'm afraid."

"Weren't you working in the storeroom here late last night?"

A subtle change came over his face. "Here? No. You must have been mistaken."

"I wasn't mistaken, Mr. Morfitt. I heard someone moving about. When I went to investigate, whoever it was had gone. They'd had to unbolt the front door to get out, so you see, there's no doubt about it at all."

"Ah . . ." He took down his white coveralls from the hook behind the counter and began to put it on, one sleeve, then the other, very slowly. When he turned back to her, he had put on his smile as well. "No need to worry. I think I know who it was. I've let one of the storerooms. It'll have been the man who's taken it, I expect. Mr. Robinson."

"Oh, I see." She should have felt relief. It was the rational explanation she had hoped for, but there was something funny about it. Something about the way Mr. Morfitt had brought it out. Why was he acting so shiftily?

"Is this Mr. Robinson going to be in and out of the storeroom a lot?" she asked.

"I don't really know, Miss Davidge. I didn't ask." More often than not Mr. Morfitt called her Julie.

"What is he storing down there?"

"Electrical stuff, I believe. It's only a short let. He won't be wanting it for long. He's moving into a new shop, and this is until he makes the move. He's short of space at the moment, you see. He's perfectly all right, I assure you. You've probably seen him about as a matter of fact. He's been in the shop several times this past week."

He was doing some natty work with the broom again, jabbing and twirling it into inaccessible corners. *He's acting like a butler who's been caught selling off the whiskey*, Julie thought. *What's the matter with him? What is there to be jumpy about in letting a storeroom?* And then she realized what it must be. He wasn't supposed to sublet. If he had the same sort of lease she had, he couldn't sublet any part of his premises without getting the landlord's permission first. And why wouldn't he ask the landlord? Because he was charging an exorbitant rent for the cellar. Now he was afraid she might tell on him. He was a greedy man.

"They're not stolen goods down there, are they, Mr. Morfitt?" she asked.

He looked quite aghast. "Good heavens, no. I assure you, nothing like that. He's a perfectly respectable businessman. You'll have to meet him, see for yourself. But he'll only be here for a short while, anyway. Just until his shop's ready."

"Well, could you ask him to make it clear when he's working late?" Julie said. "He frightened me last night. And if he unbolts the front door after I've locked up for the night and I don't know about it, it makes the house unsafe. He was here very late last night."

"I'll certainly tell him. I'll tell him it's a condition of the let that he's out by eight at the latest. Will that do?"

She nodded. "All right."

He had recovered. "Can't have you being frightened, Julie."

She did not respond.

"Any complaint from you, I'll tell him, and out he goes." He gave her a jovial smile. "Anything you want while you're here? Butter, eggs, bread?"

Julie had the feeling he would pile the whole shop in her arms, and even forget to put it on the bill, to get her to drop the subject. She shook her head and went out. She had the parting shot as she went up the stairs. "I hope the stuff he's got down there isn't inflammable. I hope you're well insured, Mr. Morfitt."

Everything was explained; everything, she supposed, was all right, but Mr. Morfitt had taken away the cozy feeling she had always enjoyed of the house belonging to her when its visitors departed at six every night. It was no longer hers alone. She knew she wouldn't be at ease in the house again at night until Mr. Robinson had gone.

Julie spent most of that day in the Victoria and Albert Museum working on costume sketches. At about four she called in at her agent's to talk about future work and was reminded of a cocktail party she had been invited to that evening. It was being held by the public relations firm of a company she had once illustrated a brochure for at the beginning of her free-lance career. They had invited her to a party at the time, and she had been asked to every one they held since. She presumed she was on some tattered list of names that was dug out on these occasions and which nobody ever bothered to alter. She hadn't been to the last three parties, but today she was unsettled and felt like going. It would stop her sitting in her flat listening for Mr. Robinson. Also she felt like buying something new, and the party was a good excuse. Nervousness always brought out in her a rash of expenditure.

She went to a small boutique she knew of near the flat. It consisted of one room on the ground floor so small you had to turn sideways to get past the counter, and a red-papered cellar downstairs crammed with clothes racks and girls and women in various stages of undress. There was no changing room and no assistant. In the dim light of the Chinese paper lanterns you rummaged through the clothes till you found what you wanted, tried it on, and took it upstairs to pay for it. It was quite a good system from the point of view of the management, Julie supposed. They didn't have to pay for assistants, and it cut down on shoplifting. Anyone stuffing six dresses into a handbag or putting one dress on top of another would be exposed to the fascinated gaze of all the other customers and could be ambushed with ease at the top of the one narrow staircase.

Whether the system worked as well for the customer was another matter. It was quite possible to find when you got out into the street that the colors of a garment were horrifyingly different from the ones that gleamed so seductively down in the Oriental interior; and after one experience of coming apart in public, Julie always got out her ancient sewing machine as soon as she got home with one of these dresses and went over all the main seams herself. But the clothes were dirt cheap and the fashion always of that very week, and that was the great attraction.

Julie spent a delightful half hour there, only complicated by the necessity of keeping her handbag more or less attached to her for safety as she stripped dresses off and on. Though she tried on several for the amusement of it, there was never any doubt about which one she would buy. It was the only one which fulfilled the two essentials of the ideal dress. It looked as good from the back as the front and she felt like a knockout in it. She paid for it and took it home. It looked just as good in the daylight, and when she examined the seams, she found them for once quite reliable.

She cleaned off her makeup and made herself a cup of tea. Then refreshed, she began to get ready.

It was one of those occasions in which getting dressed begins to develop into an act of war, with clothes and scents and makeup the weapons of defense. Like a knight caparisoning himself in armor before a battle, she chose to wear the sandals studded with *diamanté* which were really quite unsuitable for an unimportant cocktail party but which made her feet look narrow and elegant and which made her feel protected. She dusted off her hairpiece and sat with teeth against lip devising an elaborate arrangement of her hair that made her arms ache, and used up half a tin of lacquer to make it stay in place. She thought at first false eyelashes might be too much, but she tried them, batting coyly at herself in the mirror, and left them on. She zipped on the dress and sprayed herself liberally with scent.

She knew exactly what she was doing. There is still little defense a woman has against the uncertainties of the world but her confidence, and little better way of bolstering that confidence than by making herself look beautiful. It is for themselves that most women dress, not for others. On the exploitation of such fundamental truths are fortunes made.

Stephen, Richard, Dorothy, the secretive Mr. Robinson, Julie needed a defense against them all. In the past two days she had become involved with a man about whom she knew nothing but what he chose to tell her, had suffered the shock of her brother's return and the further shock of his apparent strangeness, and had had the security of her own small castle threatened. No wonder she kept on her eyelashes.

The offices the party was being held in were early Festival Hall, all glass and metal, tarnishing a little at the edges. The plastic furniture, well in advance of fashion a few years before, was beginning to look just a trifle tatty. The indoor plants, rioting up the bamboo room dividers, were of the wrong genus, and the low award-winning tables caught your shins in the crowd. There was quite a large crowd. Julie, guided to the proper room by the swelling seashell noise of a party well under way, a combination of rising shrieks over a solid ground base of male voices, found she was one of the last arrivals. It must be a quarterly, get-rid-of-the-hospitality-debt affair, she decided, for there seemed to be hundreds of people but no particular center, no signs of one product or one celebrity being pushed with free drinks and professional bonhomie. A hired waiter in a short white jacket approached her with a tray of drinks. She accepted a glass, moved a little farther into the room, and looked around.

The first person she saw, partly concealed until then by the fat green fingers of a towering rubber plant, was Michael Brent. He was talking with great animation to two attentive men who—from the cut of their suits and the courteously inclining heads, the profiles rubbed smooth of all offensive angles and sharpnesses like pebbles polished by endless waves of good relations—must have been two of the hosts. Michael glanced around, cigarette waving as he looked for an ashtray, and saw Julie. He gave her a wave of delighted surprise. The two men following his glance gazed at her with unconcealed interest. She gave them a friendly smile and inclined her head. They nodded back, expressions brightening.

Michael spoke to them, clearly detaching himself from the conversation, and came over to Julie. The men lifted their shoulders in the slightest of resigned shrugs and drifted off to other duties.

"My god, Julie," Michael said, "you're looking ravishing. What are you doing in this *galère?*"

"Passing an idle evening. And don't tell me I should be working."

"I wouldn't dream of it. Is that all your own hair?"

She put a hand to her head. "Is it falling off already?"

He laughed. "No, of course not. It looks wonderful. Who are you with?"

"I'm not with anybody. I came on my own."

"That sounds very pathetic. I came on my own, too, but I had an ulterior motive. See her, over there by the window. That gorgeous creature in blue."

Julie saw a statuesque blonde with blank blue eyes. She turned back to Michael and smiled.

"Oh, I know, I know, I've got some vulgar tastes. And I've run into difficulties. She's married, which isn't important, but her husband is here, which is. However, just before you arrived I'd coaxed her into making a lunch date with me. She thinks I can help her, you see. She has literary ambitions."

"I don't believe a word of it!"

"Still, it's worth thinking about, isn't it? What are you drinking? Your glass is empty."

"I thought it was a gin and tonic, but I think I've arrived at the time they stop putting the gin in. It's very pleasant, though. I'll have another."

"Julie, since we're both on our own, how about coming and having a meal with me? You don't want to stay here, do you? It's a bear fight. Unless there's someone you've come to see."

"No, I'd love to have dinner with you."

"Good. There's a place in Soho I go to sometimes to cheer up the owner. He was doing very well until about a year ago when two strip clubs opened up on either side of his restaurant. Now his entrance is flanked by enormous portraits of gigantic beckoning nudes; the customers who come to eat are put off their food by the sight of all those bosoms, and the others just sit there, with folded arms, waiting for the show to start. The poor man is in despair."

"I dont believe a word of that, either."

"Well, perhaps I won't take you to that one. Now there's another one I'm fond of . . . "

They went to Soho in the end, to a restaurant specializing in fish, and indulged themselves with shellfish and brown bread and butter and a light Italian wine.

"Have you noticed that whenever I take you out," Michael observed, "we spend all our time eating?"

"You always give me such good food," Julie said.

"I'm afraid it's more significant than that," he said. "I'm afraid it means we're friends."

"Oh, Michael, that's a terrible thing to say."

"Oh, I'm not disappointed. One day, when we're both old and gray, our underlying passion for each other will spring to the surface, and we'll fall rheumatically into each other's arms in a delirious extravaganza of ancient love."

"I can hardly wait."

He smiled. "You're a nice girl, Julie. And not a bad illustrator."

"Michael, I think I'm in love."

"About time, too. I thought there was something different about you. Who is he?"

"I don't know anything about him. I only met him on Monday."

"Well, don't let him put you off your work. You've got a deadline to keep."

She hesitated. "Can I tell you something very confidential?"

"As long as it's not the details of your sex life, yes."

"Richard's back."

He paused, his hand on the glass, and looked at her with alert, sharp eyes. "When?"

"Monday. At least that's when I heard. He's been here a week. He was exchanged. I don't know who for. They're keeping it quiet. Dorothy says he's ill, but I've got an instinct it's more than that. He doesn't want to see anyone."

"I should think he's exhausted, isn't he?" Michael said. "Anyway, I don't suppose they'll want him to see anyone. They'll be busy getting all the information they can out of him. That in itself would be tiring for him."

"Mike, you don't think they'll send him off again, do you?"

"I shouldn't think he'd be any use in the field now he's known. But they'll probably give him a job at home if he's fit and they don't think he's been brainwashed."

She shook her head. "I hadn't thought of that. Do you

think they've damaged his mind? The way Dorothy went on, it sounded as if he'd been turned into a half-wit."

"Dorothy is an ignorant cow. He probably acted stupidly to get rid of her. He couldn't stand her five years ago, and I shouldn't think he's changed." He put a hand comfortingly over hers. "Don't worry about him. He'll be all right. Don't think about it until you've seen him for yourself."

"I wonder how long they're going to keep it a secret that he's back. Aren't you surprised the other side hasn't let it out? I thought they always did. As a kind of victory for them."

"Your knowledge of the spy game sounds as about as authentic as mine," Michael said. "All garnered from the Sunday magazines. I should think in all probability Richard was never a spy in anybody's pay. He's got picked up by mistake, and it's taken them three years to admit they were wrong. Just the sort of thing that happens in bureaucracies. In which case the mood your sister-in-law encountered was no doubt suppressed fury at the incompetence of everybody concerned."

It was an idea she found oddly comforting. And really it was a far more believable explanation than anything else that had been put forward. One's relatives, after all, didn't become spies. That happened to other people.

Chapter 3

~~~~~~

On Thursday morning Julie had a visitor. She was expecting the laundryman, so when her bell rang, she called out. "The door's open. It's in the hall with the money on top. Leave the change on the table, please."

There was a silence, followed after a moment by a deprecatory cough.

"Miss Davidge?"

She turned from the drawing board, brushing back a trailing thread of hair. She recognized the man who stood rather diffidently at the door immediately, not personally but as a member of his group. He was wearing an extremely well-cut pinstriped suit, and his shoes were beautifully polished.

"Oh," she said. "You're one of them, aren't you?"

He came a few steps forward into the room. "I'd prefer you to have put that some other way, Miss Davidge. It makes me sound like something dropped from a flying saucer."

"Have you left your umbrella in the hall?"

He raised an eyebrow. "My umbrella?"

"The others always carried umbrellas. Everywhere."

He smiled gently. "I get the impression you're not terribly fond of us, Miss Davidge."

"Would you be?"

"Well, we did get him back."

"If it wasn't for you, he wouldn't have been there in the first place."

He sighed. His voice was soft and rather precise. "Your brother is a very patriotic man, Miss Davidge. That's a heresy here now; though transferred to emergent nations, the same people who condemn it here can hardly overpraise it, even to the extent of helping them murder one another in its name. But that's by the way. Your brother is also a very brave man, and what is more important a very professional man, and I'm extremely glad we've got him back, even if you do consider the whole affair, as I believe you do, as smacking somewhat too much of the uncultured diplomacy of more primitive times. Kidnap and ransom, mm? It's a savage world still, I'm sorry to say."

"Good heavens," Julie said. She smiled at him. "I like you a lot better after that, Mr.—"

He bowed slightly. "Holbrook. David Holbrook." He sat down rather primly on the edge of a chair. "Do you think it quite wise to leave your flat door open?"

"I shut it when I'm not here."

He opened his mouth as if to speak, looked at her, then closed it again firmly. "Mmmm," he said.

Julie left the table and came to sit opposite him. "Would you like a cup of coffee, Mr. Holbrook?"

"No, thank you."

"You have come about Richard, haven't you?"

"Of course. You want to see him, naturally."

"Dorothy did telephone you, then. His wife," she explained.

"Possibly. I don't know."

"You're not here because of anything she said then?"

"No." He paused, a delicate line of impatience beginning to crease his brow. "Well, do you want to see your brother?"

"You mean I can?"

"I've come to take you to see him."

"Now?"

"If you wish."

The doorbell rang.

"Oh, damn, that's the laundry." She raised her voice. "The door's open!"

"I'm afraid it's not," Holbrook said apologetically. "I

closed it. These old houses echo so much, don't you find? Voices carry."

Julie handed over the bundle of linen and the money and received her clean laundry and change back. She took the bundle into her bedroom. She sat down on the bed and looked at her reflection in the mirror. She was aware as never before of the way in which her life had been changed by what had happened to Richard, and particularly by the events of the past few days. Suspicion was becoming her companion. She should, as Mr. Holbrook had said, as Stephen had told her to, have locked her door. David Holbrook might not then be sitting in the other room waiting for her. How did she know where he might take her? Who could she ring up and appeal to to verify that he was who he said he was? As it happened, he had not specifically claimed to be anyone. There had only been that first moment of conviction when he entered the room that he was one of those men from one of those so ambiguous government departments that have such undefined powers and dislike publicity so much.

There comes a time, she thought, *when you have to trust your own judgment, when you must close your eyes and let your instinct rule you. There is no one to help you.*

She decided to go with him. But she did not tell him about the postcard from France. She took it from the drawer, where she had been keeping it, and thrust it deep into the pocket of her coat.

When she went back to the living room, David Holbrook was on his feet, examining one of the pictures that lay propped against the wall.

"Very interesting," he said. "What's the medium? *Gouache?*"

She looked over his shoulder. "Yes."

"Very effective." He replaced it carefully. "Shall we go?"

There were no parking meters on the street where Julie lived, only fat yellow lines running parallel to each pavement. Holbrook had been away from his car barely ten minutes, but already the insidious white notice was clinging like a parasite to his windshield wiper. He settled Julie into the passenger seat before he removed the paper, tossing it casually into the glove compartment.

"Aren't you immune from them?" Julie remarked. "Haven't you got a little card somewhere telling the traffic wardens you're on their side?"

He pursed his lips. "Well, let's put it that I might not personally pay every parking fine I incur." He started the engine and put the car into gear. "But they all do get paid." He glanced at her. "I'm glad I'm not an enemy of yours, Miss Davidge. It's hard work being your friend."

She waited until they had left the side streets and eased their way into the main body of the traffic before she spoke again. Then she apologized.

"I'm sorry if I seem snappy, Mr. Holbrook. I'm nervous."

"There's no need to be."

"I don't know what to expect."

"Your brother is perfectly all right. A little tired, of course."

"His wife said—" She broke off. "I thought we were going to Hampstead."

"Did you?"

"We've turned off."

He had swung the car smoothly around the confusing medley of new roadways at the top of Tottenham Court Road, and now they were heading east toward the City. Before long he had turned off again and yet again.

"It's exactly like being driven by an unscrupulous taxi driver," Julie commented. "Going all around London to get to the next street. Would you please tell me where we're going?"

He gave her a surprisingly reassuring smile. "I realize that this must seem very cloak and dagger. I do apologize. I merely wanted to see if anyone was interested enough to follow us."

"And were they?"

He didn't reply.

"I don't understand," she said. "If they let Richard go of their own accord, why should they still be interested in him? Unless you mean he's a lamb to catch a tiger."

"Goat."

"I beg your pardon?"

"I believe it's goats they stake out to catch tigers."

They were now back at Holborn. They appeared to be coming around in a great circle. The car slowed as the light turned red.

She looked at Holbrook curiously. "Do you know Richard well, Mr. Holbrook?"

"No, not personally." He rested his hands on the wheel, the wrists loose. "There was one man I would have said knew him very well indeed, but he's dead. He died of a heart attack a year ago. I think the news has upset your brother. I only tell you to help you understand his state of mind."

He was giving her exactly the same warning as Dorothy, only in a slightly more subtle way. She didn't ask any more questions.

She was beginning to wonder why she was being taken to see Richard at all. It would not be, she was quite sure, out of consideration for family affection.

"He's not at Hampstead, by the way," Holbrook said. "He was only staying there temporarily. He's at Regent's Park."

"His old flat?"

He nodded. "Delightful area."

"His wife told me it had been let."

"Oh, we took care of it for him. We never, you see, Miss Davidge, quite abandoned him."

Richard's flat was not in the most expensive and carefully kept-up part of Regent's Park, but it was very pleasant all the same. It gave Julie the first sense of reality in the whole affair to be able to step once again into his black-and-white tiled hall and to see a coat of his hanging up on the old-fashioned coat rack he had brought from the family house when it was sold, along with the antique table and the vast set of glass-fronted bookcases which now lined his living room.

The shock was for that reason all the greater when she entered the familiar oblong room with its tall sash windows, full of a gentle green light reflected from the burgeoning trees outside, and saw the man sitting in Richard's chair. Her first thought was that it couldn't be Richard, and then she remembered the photograph of him published in the newspapers some months before. The man in the photograph, hollow-cheeked, ill, with the blank eyes of exhaustion, was the same man who now got to his feet and stood watching her. She thought at first they had broken his nose and then realized he had lost so much weight that all the bones in his face were revealed in a way she had never seen them. The suit he was wearing hung on him in folds, and that, quite as much as the physical change, made him look different. In clothes that fitted him he would have been more recognizable.

He seemed to be waiting for her to speak.

"If this is what you look like after a week's feeding up," she said, "I'm glad I didn't see you when you arrived."

At that he threw back his head and laughed in a way so completely his own that she felt an upsurge of relief and affection for him.

"Julie," he said simply, and he looked at once more human and more relaxed. The lines of his face which had been, until she spoke, taut with some inner tension, eased and softened. It was going to be possible after all to accept this stranger as Richard.

They had never been close, even in childhood, especially in childhood when the difference in age had been a barrier as great as their fundamental difference in temperament. He had always been bold, adventurous, extremely self-assured, whereas Julie, in everything but the practice of her craft, was a drifter and a dreamer. Richard planned meticulously; she acted more often than not purely on impulse. They did not even look alike. As is so often the case with a brother and sister, she resembled her father, whereas Richard was a masculine version of their mother. The only qualities they shared were the professionalism of their attitude toward their work and a certain stubbornness of character. They were not easily shifted from a course they had chosen.

Julie suspected that to Richard, taking over parental responsibility for her at the death of her parents, she would always be a child, and she found herself too often at their occasional meetings reacting in the way he expected, as if in some conspiracy to maintain the fiction. With him she spoke more impulsively, her views became too emphatic, her proclaimed judgments obviously immature, even her vocabulary had a way of slipping back into the schoolroom. Above the solid basis of loyalty and affection that both unconsciously accepted as an irremovable part of the structure of their lives, they were, in the ordinary commerce of life, rather awkward with each other.

"Julie," Richard said. "You haven't changed. You look very pretty. No need to tell me how I look. Everyone winces in horror at me." He held out a hand to her. "Come over here, sit down, tell me what you've been doing since you left college. Dorothy said you're making a lot of money. Are you still in that decrepit old flat?"

"Richard, I believe you've developed a foreign accent."

"That's quite probable. After hearing no English for three years, it's rather like speaking a foreign language."

She sat down beside him and searched in her handbag for a handkerchief.

"Oh, no," he said. "Now, come on, dear, don't start crying. You're a big girl now."

She blew her nose. "Well, it's not surprising, is it? My

long-lost brother. And you look so awful. When I think what they've done to you, I hate them all, your David Holbrooks as well as those horrible people over there."

"Now shut up. Just be glad I'm back. Have a cigarette—I've got some somewhere."

Everything he said was spoken jerkily, with quick phrases followed by pauses, as if he were breathless or as if he had to concentrate very hard.

"Are they Dorothy's?" she said.

He looked puzzled.

"She told me you'd pinched hers."

"Oh, yes. No, I finished those." He found a pack on the mantelpiece. "Here we are. And a match, too." He lit the cigarette for her.

"Have you given up your pipes?" she asked.

He cupped his hands around his face, lighting his own cigarette. His hands, she noticed, were trembling slightly.

"I've got used to cigarettes," he said after a pause. "Though even these give me palpitations now."

"Richard, how are you, really?"

"They tell me I've got no diseases that can't be cured."

"Don't be so flippant about it. Was that why they let you go? Because you're ill?"

He patted her hand. "No, I don't think so. I don't know why they let me go. To improve their image, perhaps. It happened so quickly and unexpectedly, in the way these things do. One day I was suddenly hauled out of the camp and taken to the capital. They gave me a bed with a pillow to sleep on and the next day drove me to a bridge on the frontier and told me to get out and start walking. The guards walked behind me. I thought at first I was going to be shot. Then I saw this car waiting on the other side and a group of men coming toward us. I wouldn't believe what was happening, not until I was in the car and driving away."

"The man who was exchanged for you—"

He interrupted her. "I didn't know him. It was no one very important, I'm told. Unflattering, in a way. And after two years of blank refusal even to discuss an exchange, overtures suddenly came from the other side. It's puzzling. That's why my friends here kept me incommunicado for a week, while they asked their questions. They were still trying to work out if it's an isolated instance or a change of policy. I shouldn't be talking to you so freely, of course, but I don't give a damn. The place will be humming with bugs, anyway."

She was astonished. "This flat, you mean? But why?"

He shrugged. "No one trusts anyone these days."

She realized he was deadly serious.

"Do you," she asked, "trust anyone?"

He drew in a lungful of smoke and exhaled it slowly. "No. And they don't trust me. They've got a watchdog downstairs, did Holbrook tell you?"

"I thought there was a young couple living in the flat below."

"They've gone. They've got a man of their own there now. Where is Holbrook, by the way?"

"He let me in and then he went down to wait in the car."

"Very sensitive of him."

"You don't like him?"

He shrugged again, without speaking. He looked very tired. The animation of those first few minutes had been only a spurious vitality. It had been fading as he talked. Even the company of a sister, even for so short a time, was almost too much for him. She ought to go.

"Richard, if you stay here in your own flat, won't the news get out that you're back?"

"Yes, I expect it will."

"Won't that mean newspapers and TV people coming here? Are you fit enough to deal with them?"

"I didn't like the place I was in. I told them I wanted to sleep in my own bed, and I'm damned well going to."

"Oh, that sounds like you!"

"That's an odd thing to say. Don't I sound like myself?"

"Yes, of course you do."

He moved over to the fireplace. "It won't be necessary to spend a lot of time on the press. When they get wind of what's happened, I suppose there'll be some kind of conference. I shall tell them I'm very glad to be home and that I intend to start rebuilding my business. No doubt they will ask me if I mean to go abroad again, and I shall say, in a dry way, 'not in the near future,' and a ripple of amused sympathy will spread around the assembly, and that will be all that's necessary." He smiled at her. "That shouldn't tire me out."

She smiled back. She wanted to hug him. She had never been so fond of him.

"After that," he said, "or even before, as soon as possible in fact, I think I'd like to go fishing somewhere. Ireland, perhaps. I have lapses of memory, you know, Julie. I imagine it's a condition that will improve in time, but it's disconcerting. It alarms 'them.' I believe they're wondering what I'm concealing." He had not changed the tone of his voice, but the tension was there again and growing. "They see before them a broken man, and they don't like the smell of him."

"You didn't break."

"They didn't expect me to plead guilty. They know how it's done. A man can be mentally confused by drugs, isolation, starvation, and so on, until he doesn't know what he's saying, but they didn't expect that of me. What they don't understand is that I did not do it. I never pleaded guilty or signed anything. A plea was entered for me. There were no observers in that court. They could put whatever words they liked into my mouth. Now they prefer to believe those lies instead of me."

She wondered if this was the source of the strain he was enduring. Did his lapses of memory cover the time of the trial? Had he forgotten exactly what had happened? Was he worrying that he had, in fact, pleaded guilty? What did it matter? she thought. Why should he have to torture himself about it? She felt full of indignation and pain for him.

"I was going to make an attempt to escape, you know. Before I got too weak to walk."

"Does anyone ever escape from those camps?"

"It's possible to get out of them. It's getting away from them and staying alive as far as the frontier that's the problem. Though there are people who will help now, here and there, if you can find them." He bent down and switched on the electric heater that stood in front of the empty grate. "I get cold so easily." He glanced around at her. "I would have got away. I would have done it."

"Yes," she said. "Yes, Richard."

He went on talking, telling her scraps of his story, breaking off abruptly, beginning again, circling restlessly around the subject of his trial. He would try to talk about Julie's life in London, speaking normally, wittily, for a while, and then he would fall silent and seem to forget her, returning to the prison in his mind. He would become agitated and light a cigarette with frail fingers, sucking the smoke in as if only that could sustain him.

But it was the room, more than anything, Julie thought, which was helping him maintain his balance. He would look around at it, as if drawing strength from every familiar surface and object, from the realization that he was where he was and not where, waking, he must most fear to be.

Julie understood now too well what had upset Dorothy, what Holbrook had meant by his warning about Richard's state of mind. She did not understand why they should be surprised. Did they expect such an experience to leave a man unchanged? What he needed was peace and quiet and food and rest and no one to worry him. He knew it himself. Fishing in Ireland. They should let him go at once. She had an almost maternal feeling for him. She wanted to protect him.

She hesitated, she hesitated for a long time before she brought up the matter of the postcard that had arrived from France. Eventually, when he seemed calmer, she said, "The day I heard you were back, Richard, someone sent me a postcard you had written to me when you were in Lyons." She held it out to him, and he took it indifferently.

"Did I send you a postcard? That was unusually fraternal of me."

"Don't you remember it?" She realized at once she should not have phrased it that way. She should not have given him one more incident to strain his mind over. It was obvious he had forgotten it.

He turned the card over in his hand as if willing himself to remember it. "It's a long time ago."

"Yes, of course it is. It doesn't matter." She made herself go on. "Do you remember a man called Stephen Archer?"

He looked across at her, frowning. "Stephen who?"

"Archer. It was in Lyons."

"Why? Is it important?"

"No. I met him once; he asked about you, that's all." She would do nothing to upset him. She took the card back and put it in her pocket. "Are you feeling any warmer? Why don't you put a sweater on? It would be warmer than a jacket."

He shook his head. He sat down again, close to the fire, and leaned his head on his hand. "I'm so stupidly tired. I do nothing but sleep."

"I'll go. I'll come and see you another time."

"Yes." He did not raise his head. "Another time."

She was quite fierce with Holbrook on the way back.

"Do you suspect Richard of something?" she asked him.

Holbrook glanced at her. "No."

"He believes you've got the flat wired."

"Yes, I know."

"Have you?"

"No."

He glanced in his rearview mirror and abruptly swung the car right, taking advantage of a momentary gap in the stream. It was lunchtime and the traffic was heavy. They were edging along a yard at a time in a stink of exhaust. The smell, on an empty stomach, was beginning to nauseate Julie. She said, "He worries about that plea of guilty at his trial."

"Yes, I know. It's unimportant. It doesn't matter."

"He thinks it important. He thinks you don't trust him."

Holbrook did not reply. His silence infuriated her. "You think he's suffering from persecution mania, is that it? You think he's gone mad."

"No, I think he's in the same condition as a man who's been in a bomb explosion. He's in a state of shock. But he'll get over it. You mustn't worry about it, Miss Davidge. He's only been back a week, after all."

The nausea was turning into dizziness. She fought it in silence and then asked him to pull up. She did not wish to collapse dramatically at his feet. "I'm a little faint," she explained.

He was immediately both alarmed and solicitous. "I'm terribly sorry. How thoughtless of me. I should have realized."

He threaded through the traffic to the left-hand pavement and stopped the car. Julie leaned forward with her head against the dashboard.

"It's been a terrible shock for you, too," Holbrook said. "Let me get you a drink, a brandy or something. There's a pub on the next corner."

She shook her head. "I'm all right now." She smiled weakly at him. "Besides, you couldn't leave the car. You'd get another ticket."

"Then I'll get you home as quickly as I can. I can take a shortcut from here."

She sat with her eyes closed for the last stage of the journey. She was drained of all energy. Reaction, she supposed. Like Richard, she could sleep for a week. She became aware of her surroundings again when they were outside Mr. Morfitt's shop. Holbrook was regarding her with definite signs of anxiety. "Are you all right, Miss Davidge? Do you want anyone fetched?"

"I'm much better. Don't worry. Thank you for your kindness." She fumbled with the catch, and Holbrook leaned across her and opened the door.

"If you're sure you're all right, I won't get out. If you don't mind. If you're quite sure."

Men like him always protested too much. They wore you out with their concern.

"Are you going to let Richard hold a press conference?" she asked him.

She could sense his relief at her return to normal. "If necessary. We won't let him be badgered." He gave her one of his reassuring smiles. "We'll keep the publicity to a minimum. Get it over with next week perhaps, then let him get off to Ireland for his fishing."

She nodded and thanked him. She got out and shut the car door and watched him drive away. She was wondering if today was the first time Richard had talked about going to Ireland; if Holbrook had waited in the car, as he said; or if he had been in the flat below Richard's, with the watchdog, listening.

Coming upstairs at two o'clock the next day, her arms full of a new supply of working materials, Julie found Miss Margery Dawson, the head of the three-woman typing agency on the top floor, poised outside their communal lavatory door in a visible state of rage.

With her permed head and clothes that were not so much a defiance of fashion as an inability to recognize that things had changed since she was eighteen and bought her first "smart" suit with her saved-up clothing coupons, Miss Dawson had always seemed to Julie a classic case of a certain kind of single woman, encased in a rigid shell of her own contriving that protected her from those aspects of life, such as politics, revolutions, abstract thought, and sex, that she did not wish to think about and which enabled her to live comfortably and enjoyably within the narrow confines of her job, her small flat in Sidcup, and her annual coach trip to the Continent with a widowed school friend who was glad of the company; a very unlikely person, in fact, to display this sort of fundamental impatience on a public staircase.

Deciding that even a nod might not be diplomatic at this juncture, Julie was passing her by as if she were invisible when a hissed exclamation startled her to a halt.

"He's in there again! Did you know?"

Julie turned. "Who?"

Miss Dawson bent toward her conspiratorially, her voice a hoarse whisper. "That friend of Mr. Morfitt's. The one who's renting a storeroom. He's always doing it."

Julie found herself whispering back. "Perhaps he doesn't know there's one downstairs."

"Then Mr. Morfitt must tell him. One wouldn't mind so much if he wasn't so ill-mannered about it. He pushed past me just now, simply pushed me aside. I wonder you didn't hear the noise as you came in. And Denise said yesterday he rushed down past her, nearly knocking her over the banister, and slammed the door in her face. So rude. It was just as you came in, when you were feeling faint. How are you now, dear?"

Denise, another member of the agency, had seen Julie leaning against the wall in a groggy way on her return from seeing Richard and had kindly made her a cup of tea.

"Oh, I'm fine now, thank you," she said.

"That's good. But there you are, I mean, you might have been, well, in need, mightn't you? And it is the 'ladies' after all. I'm thinking of putting a notice on it. It's the pushing and the rudeness of it, you see. I mean, if Mr. Robinson suffers from some complaint, I'm sympathetic, but he should use the downstairs, really he should."

She glanced over her shoulder at the closed door. "He's not coming out till we've gone," she whispered. "I suppose he can hear us talking. Well, I'm going straight down to Mr. Morfitt to complain. No matter how unpleasant it is, we must get it settled once and for all."

She went determinedly down the stairs.

Julie did not wait to hear the results of the confrontation. She was quite sure Miss Dawson would win the day because of Mr. Morfitt's extreme sensitivity to complaints about his tenant.

She was, at that point, merely amused by the incident. The Mr. Robinson who had become involved in this domestic complication was much more acceptable to her than the mysterious creature who had lurked in secret and sinister fashion in the cellar that night. It made him human and forgettable.

She put away her materials in a methodical fashion and set herself to consider with critical care her latest piece of work. The previous evening she had completed a new illustration commissioned by Michael Brent. She had still had plenty of time before it was due, but the unease which now dwelled constantly beneath the surface of her mind had seemed to act as a stimulus.

About six she had rung up Richard to see how he was and had heard a definite click on the line as if it were tapped. As a result she had said very little to him, and he had been equally unresponsive. It had been an unsatisfactory conversation. He sounded strange on the phone, distant and unlike himself. She had put the receiver down and got on with her work and stayed with it until it was finished. And now this afternoon when she looked at it again, she wasn't displeased. She decided to take it around to the publisher's office before she felt impelled to make changes that would inevitably involve her in redoing the whole thing.

Anne Latham, Michael's secretary, was sitting alone at her desk in his office doing her household accounts. She pulled a face at Julie. "He's out. With his latest blonde. Lunch at one and now it's"—she looked at her watch—"four o'clock. Do you want to wait?"

"Is it worth it?" Julie asked.

Anne shrugged. "He might not come back at all."

Julie smiled. "Well, anyway, here's the illustration. May I leave it?"

"Yes, of course. I'll take good care of it. What shall we do? Shall we ring you or will you ring us?"

"I'll ring you. How's your husband?"

A grin spread over Anne's round face. "Getting fat. I'm making sure he hasn't got the speed to chase blondes."

Julie went back to the ground floor in the lift and regretted it when the lift bounced twice before coming to rest. She pulled the heavy iron gates open and shut with difficulty. As usual there was no one in the entrance hall to give her a hand. As soon as the contact was made, the lift gave an alarming rattle and began creaking slowly upward again on its ancient pulleys. Some members of the staff, at least, still had faith in it.

On her way back to the flat, she stopped in at the Morfitts to buy some frozen fish. Mrs. Morfitt served her. In the far corner of the shop, near the door leading to the back rooms, Mr. Morfitt was talking to another man. The man had his back to Julie. He looked around when she came in, then turned away again as if uninterested.

Julie took her fish and went upstairs. She passed the door of her own flat and went on up the final flight to the offices of the typing agency. They had two small rooms and an antechamber which were situated immediately above her own. Miss Dawson, as the head, had one room to herself; Denise and Janet, her two assistants, shared the larger one. When Julie went in, they were all sitting in the bigger room. They had just done their post and were having a last cup of coffee.

"Has Mr. Robinson got a widow's peak?" Julie asked.

They looked at her with some astonishment. Julie had noticed before that if you ask people an unexpected, direct question no matter how flutingly clear your voice may be, they don't appear to hear you. She repeated her question.

"Yes, now you mention it, he has," Miss Dawson said.

"His hair's very greasy," Denise said. "Ugh, horrible."

"He's inoffensive," Miss Dawson said. "but not very clean." She nodded meaningfully at Julie. "I spoke to Mr. Morfitt." She had evidently won hands down.

"Oh, good," Julie said.

"Why did you ask about his hair?"

"I wanted to make sure it was the same man. I saw him in the shop on Monday, before I knew about the storeroom. And he's down there now. I was curious." He had been in the cinema, too, she had remembered, the same day, the day the postcard came from France.

"Those two occasions," she said delicately, "when he pipped you at the post, had he been up here to see you?"

They regarded her with further astonishment. "No. Why do you think that?"

"Well, you said, Miss Dawson, that he pushed past you, and you, Denise, that he rushed *down* past you. The lavatory is on the first floor landing, so that if he was coming *down* to it he must have been coming from here or—"

"Or from your flat," Miss Dawson finished for her.

Janet, the youngest and most down-to-earth of the three, spoke for the first time.

"Well, he hasn't been here," she stated. "Not either time."

There was a short silence. Denise, a tall busty girl with intricately styled hair, sucked her breath in sibilantly. "Perhaps he's a thief."

"Has your lock been tampered with?" Miss Dawson asked.

"He wouldn't need to," Denise said. "They use keys."

"I don't see anything's gone," Julie said. "I haven't noticed."

"I should have a good look when you go down," said Miss Dawson. "I don't know about Mr. Morfitt, I'm sure, letting people like that into the house."

"Perhaps he didn't get into your flat," Janet suggested. "Perhaps he was disturbed."

Denise leaned forward, her face flushed with excitement. "That's it! That's what he was up to. He must have been trying to get into your flat each time when he heard you coming. It was to avoid you catching him at your door. He didn't want you to see him. So he rushed down and jumped in the toilet to hide. You want to watch out he doesn't try a third time."

"But I've got nothing to steal," Julie protested.

"He doesn't know that, does he?" Miss Dawson said. "Oh, I'm going to worry about you all on your own. Do you think you should get hold of the police?"

"There's nothing to tell them."

"Well, I don't know what to suggest. But if he tries anything and you catch him at it, you give us a yell. We'll get the police straightaway, never you mind, 999 at the first shout."

"Till five thirty, anyway," Janet said.

"Thank you very much," Julie said. She backed away from their absorbed and fascinated gaze. "He could have been coming up here to pinch your handbags or the petty cash," she said weakly. "At least he could get in here without breaking down doors."

"Yes, that's true. We'll have to keep an eye on our bags." They rallied cheerfully to the thought, but it was clear that in their eyes Julie was established beyond doubt as Mr. Robinson's chosen victim.

The awful thing was she felt sure they were right. She had distrusted him from the beginning, and now there was something more than instinct to go on. Had he followed her to the cinema that day or was that coincidence? Was he a petty thief or something more? A maniac who looked for lonely women in cinemas and then followed them home. And then went to the trouble of hiring storerooms at exorbitant rents, she asked herself derisively, just to get the chance to break into a flimsily locked flat to pinch a few paints and some costume jewelry? *Perhaps he's after my pictures,* she thought. *He's an art lover overwhelmed by my genius. He's seen them through the window with his long-range binoculars, and he's going to steal the lot and sell them as his own.* She felt better when she could laugh at herself.

But it was difficult to keep laughing when six o'clock came and everyone went home and the house fell into its evening silence, the silence that had once been so pleasant and was now spoiled. She wished she were ten years old and sitting in that big room with the bookcases all around, drawing pictures of horses with her colored crayons, while her mother knitted and the cat stretched and curled voluptuously before the open fire. *What I need*, she thought to herself, *is someone to look after me.* She thought of Stephen Archer and tried to re-create the intensity of communication she had felt in his presence. She could see him vividly for a moment sitting in the chair as he had done that evening, looking at her with that calm, commanding air. If he were here, he would take charge of her; he would know what to do. She felt he should be here, that it was his place to be with her. And with the thought of him, the strange, uneasy, lost feeling she had been suffering from during the past few days became identifiable. She had, in that old-fashioned phrase, been yearning for him. There was a void in her life that had not been there before she met him, but now would always be there except when he was with her. *Ring me up*, she willed him. *Ring me up, talk to me, let me know I haven't imagined you.*

He rang her up about eleven that night. When she first heard his voice, she felt amazed, as if she had conjured him up by a spell, but her mood soon changed. The call was far from reassuring. To begin with, he sounded brusque and preoccupied.

"I've just got back from Germany," he said. "Have you seen Richard?"

"Yes," Julie said. "Stephen, are you in London?"

"No, I'm ringing from my flat. I've only just got in. How is your brother?"

"Worn-out, very thin," she said. "Otherwise all right."

"Did you ask him about the cards?"

"He didn't remember anything about them. But it was a long time ago, Stephen. And his memory isn't very good."

There was a kind of sigh at the other end of the line. His voice became more urgent. "Julie, I'm not saying much now. I'll see you first thing in the morning. I'm taking the night train."

She was becoming frightened. "What is it? What's happened?"

"I got home tonight to find my post waiting for me. I've received another card. No envelope this time. Posted direct from France. Same handwriting as your card, same signature. It was posted the beginning of this week, Julie, do you understand what I'm saying?"

"Yes, yes!" She couldn't take it in, his urgency, the implications. "What does it mean?" she cried. "What's happening?"

"That," Stephen said, "is what I'm coming down to London to find out."

Chapter 4

~~~~~~

She held the postcard with both hands. She held it with extreme care, as if it were a bomb that might go off at any moment, a time bomb, which, in a way, it was.

"Do you know St. Malo?" Stephen asked.

"No," she said. "I've never been there. Do those walls go right around?"

"Around the old city? Yes."

It was an attractive card, in color, the photograph taken on a bright summer day which emphasized the contrast between the density of the towering gray walls that rose so abruptly from the rocky peninsula and the delicate clarity of the Breton sea and sky. "The ramparts at St.-Malo," it said on the reverse of the card, the printing nearly obscured by the bold scrawl of the written message: "Wish you were here!" And nothing else but the signature: "Richard."

Julie said, as she had said before, quite calmly, "What does it mean?"

Stephen sat down beside her and took the card from her hands. He clasped her hands between his and almost absent-mindedly bent his head and touched his lips to her fingers. He had been very quiet and tender with her ever since he had arrived.

"Are you sure," he said evenly, "that the man who came back, the man you saw, is your brother?"

She sighed. "I've got to face that, haven't I? That is the crux of it. I was awake all night trying to work out what it could mean, and it came down to one simple impossible question. Who is sending these cards, who is writing with Richard's writing and signing with Richard's signature?"

"Why would they do it?" he said. "And who would do it? Who knows both you and me and my brief connection with Richard?"

She said nothing. He picked the card up again. "Is this Richard's writing?"

"As far as I can judge."

"Then I think we must act as if Richard had sent it."

He had arrived at 7 A.M. on a pale morning, and she had gone down in her dressing gown to let him in. He had seemed taller than she remembered, and more solid, and when he had silently put an arm around her shoulders and hugged her to him as they walked up the stairs, there had been a warmth and a masculine assuredness about him that was more comforting than any verbal protestation of love.

"If Richard sent this, then he is in St.-Malo at this moment," Julie said. "Is that what you understand by it?"

"Yes."

"And the message: 'Wish you were here'?"

"Just what it says. He wants help."

"But how did he get to France? And why choose St.-Malo, and if he is in St.-Malo, who is the man living in his flat?"

"Let's take it a step a a time," Stephen said. "After two years of stonewalling, an exchange for your brother is suddently suggested, someone of no particular importance, quite acceptable to our side. Every door is opened, and Richard is rushed back to England. Now your brother, according to this man Holbrook you told me about, is an important agent, highly respected. Why should the other side let him go? It seems unreasonable, odd. There is one answer which, unlikely as it seems, could account for all the factors, including the postcards, and which would also explain the urgency of the transaction: if the real Richard had escaped. Suppose Richard had got away from the labor camp and the weeks had gone by and they had not recaptured him; suppose they had a man who sufficiently resembled Richard to pass for him, allowing for the changes the years of imprisonment could be assumed to have made in him; then by seizing the opportunity and sending him as a substitute, they had a chance of placing a man right at the heart of our organization and at the same time blocking Richard's chance of acceptance if he did get back."

"But do you really believe such a substitution is possible?" Julie said. "How could a stranger deceive all the people who knew Richard, and never be questioned?"

"They'll have your brother's history down to the last detail. They'll have dossiers on you, on Dorothy, on everyone who knew him. They must have had tapes and films of your brother they could use. The man would have been taught how Richard spoke, rehearsed in all his mannerisms and gestures. The first meetings would have been the dangerous ones. You said yourself you didn't recognize him at first. What was it convinced you?"

"His laugh," Julie said. "His voice, his manner."

"Things that could be imitated," Stephen said. "And the situation regarding his personal relationships was all in their favor. They would know he had been separated from his wife for some time. He doesn't seem to have had any particular girlfriend at the time he vanished, certainly he had no one living with him. Even you were not especially close to him. You were told he had been exchanged, he was offered to you by the authorities as your brother, he looked like him, he talked like him—it would never occur to you to think of doubting him. As for Holbrook and his friends, naturally a man handed over in such official circumstances would be accepted. As long as the real Richard never reached England, the substitute would have little to worry about."

"He was very nervous when I first went into the room," Julie said. "I remember his hands trembled. And his voice—there was something different about it, a faint foreign intonation. He used to smoke nothing but a pipe; now he smokes cigarettes. He has lapses of memory. He seems ill and sometimes breaks off a conversation abruptly."

"Illness and loss of memory are useful defenses," Stephen said. "No one will press him too hard; all oddities of behavior will be explained by his experiences. He's all set. Dorothy's accepted him, you've accepted him—"

"They don't trust him entirely," Julie broke in. "I think that's why Holbrook took me there, to see my reactions.

Richard said they were listening in. Now I think he was right."

"Did you say anything to Holbrook afterward?"

"I attacked him for not trusting Richard."

"You see?" Stephen said. "Whoever he is, he must believe he's safely home."

Julie got up restlessly. They had been sitting with the light on. Now she pulled back the curtains and let in the day. The world outside had a drab, desolate look. She stood in front of the window and watched a black and white cat padding its self-sufficient way up the empty street. It was Saturday, she remembered. All this had happened in less than a week.

"What is the point of it, all this dangerous charade?" she said. "I understand it's not likely they'll use Richard as an active agent again."

"If the substitute is accepted and taken back into the fold, it will be a brilliant coup. They won't want him sent back into the field. They'll want him where he'll be, in London, inside, gradually reestablishing himself, gradually regaining trust. These departments are very loyal to their own men. They'll fight half his battles for him. He's a young man. They won't care how many years it takes."

"What about the real Richard? What were they going to do when he turned up?"

"The man in possession is in the strongest position. But I believe they intend to make sure he never does turn up. As soon as he puts his nose anywhere near you or Dorothy or his colleagues, they'll get him. They'll be waiting for him right now. And that's what Richard knows, too. That's what the postcards mean. They're both an establishment of identity and a call for help."

"Oh, God," she said, "if it's true, it's terrible."

"I can't think of any other rational explanation."

"I can't believe I could make such a mistake. I can't believe I wouldn't know my own brother."

"Were there any moments when you doubted him, any flickers of doubt, anything?"

"At the beginning perhaps, when I first saw him, but then when we talked—no, I don't know, I can't think! It was Richard, it must have been Richard!"

That gazing around the room, she thought, *had he been learning it rather than remembering it? That tension when* she first came in, that tense, waiting moment before she spoke, before she showed she knew him, that strange way of talking, that watchfulness, that emphasis on his loss of memory, on his lack of trust—

"I've got to see him again," she said. "I've got to know."

"It's too dangerous," Stephen said. "You might give yourself away."

"There's no other way," Julie said. "I've got to be sure."

"The only way to be sure," he said, "is to go to St.-Malo and see the man who sent this card."

She looked down at the card, its bright surface glossily shining under the electric light. She had forgotten the light. Stephen got up and switched it off. *He still reads my mind,* she thought; *I didn't imagine that.* His face was shadowed. The daylight was not yet strong enough to reach the corners of the room. She said, "Stephen—"

He came across to her and drew her away from the window. He put his arms around her, holding her so tightly she could not have moved even if she had wished to. She rested her cheek against the warmth of his shoulder.

"I don't believe anyone ever gets away from those camps," she said.

"Neither do I," Stephen said. "But it's possible. Plenty of people escaped from all sorts of unlikely places during the war, and got home."

"I'm going to see Richard again," she said, "before I do anything else. Don't stop me."

"All right."

"I'll be very careful. If it's not him, I won't let him know I know."

"Yes, all right, Julie. I understand. Perhaps it is the most sensible thing to do. If you're certain it is your brother, we'll know there must be some other explanation for the card."

He was being quietly reasonable. He wasn't leaping to wild ideas; he was considering possibilities. It should have calmed her, but it made her more frightened. It made the extraordinary seem possible, even inevitable.

And there was another factor which fitted with a nightmare logic into that unlikely pattern. There was Mr. Robinson. If Stephen's supposition was true, they would be watching for Richard, to prevent him from reaching his family and friends. Was Mr. Robinson her watcher?

She remembered Mr. Robinson in the middle of the breakfast she cooked for them, and the crash as she put her cup down sent the tea slopping into the saucer.

"What's the matter?" Stephen said.

She told him, putting in everything she knew about Mr. Morfitt's tenant, beginning with the first time she had seen him, the day the card from Lyons arrived.

"Is the grocer, what's-he-called, here today?" Stephen asked.

"He's open until twelve thirty on Saturdays."

"We'll go and see him." He smiled across the table at her. "Finish your breakfast. He'll keep a few more minutes."

As they went downstairs to the shop a little later, Julie wondered why it was that everything she did seemed muddled and erratic and everything Stephen did seemed to have an almost sublime simplicity about it. Once she had begun to think of Mr. Robinson as an enemy, she would never have dreamed of tackling Morfitt about him. She would have run a mile to avoid him. But when, after waiting until a customer had left and the grocer was alone, Stephen began to speak, she realized he was capable of a Machiavellian deviousness she would never have suspected in him.

He went straight to the point. "Miss Davidge suspects the man to whom you have let a storeroom, a Mr. Robinson, I believe, of attempting to effect an entry into her flat," he stated blandly. "Could you let me have some information about him, please?"

He made no claims, involved himself in no pretense, but the authority of his manner and the deliberate, cunning choice of words did it for him. Mr. Morfitt, assuming at once that it was an official police inquiry, visibly shrank. He darted a nervous glance at Julie.

"Oh, I am so sorry, Miss Davidge, I never thought—and Miss Dawson complained, too. But I do assure you, officer, he seemed perfectly genuine. He was very respectably dressed and quite well spoken."

Julie kept her face stiff. Stephen said simply, "Indeed."

Once started, Morfitt could not be stopped. "He came into the shop one day and asked me if I had a storeroom to let. He intimated I would be doing him a favor. He was prepared to pay"—he licked his lips and snatched another covert glance at Julie—"a very good rent for such a short let.

I only did it to oblige him, as one businessman to another. I mean, the storeroom was empty."

"What did he store there?" Stephen asked.

"Electrical equipment," he said. "I didn't see it going in. It was only until his new shop was ready. I did tell Miss Davidge." He dropped his voice. "He hasn't taken anything, has he, Miss Davidge?" Visions of court cases, eviction, ruin were evidently crowding his mind.

"I don't think so," she said.

"Oh, that's good." He cheered up considerably. "Because you've no need to worry anymore—he's gone."

"Gone?"

"Yes, I told you it was a short let. As a matter of fact, I was surprised. I didn't expect it to be quite as short as that. But he's given me a week's notice and gone."

"And taken his stuff?" Stephen asked.

"No, not yet. He's not given up the key yet, but it will all be out by next Saturday. That's definite, and when he comes to take it away, I'll see he doesn't go upstairs. You can be sure of that."

He was becoming earnestly officious. Anything to be on the right side, for Mr. Morfitt. Julie hadn't realized until this last week that he was not only greedy but a born crawler. Sometimes it was better not to learn too much about the people with whom you came in daily contact. Relationships stayed pleasanter if you never got beneath the surface.

"Do you know if he is coming himself to fetch his equipment or sending for it?" Stephen asked.

"He didn't say." Morfitt looked at him anxiously. "That is all right, isn't it, officer? Will you want me to telephone you when he comes in, if he does come in, or will you leave a man here?"

"You leave it all to us," Stephen said. "By the way, have you got an address for him?"

"No, he didn't give me one. The transaction was all—ah—verbal."

"You didn't ask for a reference?"

He shook his head. The worried look was back. Julie could feel him forcing himself not to look at her again, not to draw any more attention to himself than he could.

"Well, that will be all. Thank you very much," Stephen said, gripping Julie's arm. "But I would advise you to change the locks as soon as Robinson has handed in the keys, and

I should be a bit more careful about whom you let your storeroom to again. There are some funny characters about."

"Yes, yes, indeed. Thank you very—" They closed the door on his chattering relief.

Before they went back to the flat, Stephen went into the basement and tried the cellar doors. Both were firmly locked.

"Well?" he said when they were back in Julie's living room.

"I think Robinson's a crook with stolen property in the cellar, and he couldn't resist trying to break into the flat, out of habit."

Stephen said nothing. "Well?" she urged him.

"If he was involved in the business of Richard," he said slowly, "I don't think he would leave so soon."

"There you are," she said in relief. "There's nothing to it. Richard is sitting at home in his flat, and there's no plot."

"I don't like you living in this house, whether there's a plot or not. You're too vulnerable."

"It's not easy to find an unfurnished flat in the middle of London."

"We'll find somewhere," he said. That assumption was there again, she noticed, that "we" that took her for granted. She had either to fight it or surrender to it, and she didn't want to fight.

He kissed her lightly on the mouth. "How about making me a nice cup of coffee. I'm going to have ten minutes' sleep. I've been up all night."

He put his legs up on the sofa, closed his eyes, and went immediately to sleep with the directness with which he did everything else. He slept for an hour. Julie made the coffee and drank it herself, sitting in the chair opposite, watching him. She had a small bet with herself that when he awoke, it would be instantly, to complete comprehending consciousness. She won the bet. He opened his eyes, looked across at her, and said, "Ah, good. Coffee."

"I can see there are going to be difficulties," she said. "I usually take about an hour to come to in the mornings."

He thought her remark over and then smiled. "So do I, except when I catnap."

"Good," she said calmly, and went to make more coffee.

Julie went to Richard's flat on her own. She wouldn't let Stephen go with her even part of the way in case that made the unthinkable true. It was a kind of superstition in reverse, like taking out an umbrella in order to guarantee a sunny day.

If she took every precaution and acted as if it wasn't Richard, then it would be.

He opened the door to her himself, and she missed his first reaction to her reappearance because she was looking at the knife. He was holding it in his right hand, a long, sharp bread knife.

"Julie," he said. "I wasn't expecting you."

"Were you expecting someone else?" She nodded at the knife. He glanced down at it and laughed.

"No, as a matter of fact, I was making myself a sandwich. Come on in and have one."

She followed him into the kitchen. There was some cold ham on the table, still in its wrapping paper, and a loaf of bread and half a pound of butter.

"Have you been shopping?" she asked.

"They brought them up from downstairs." He began cutting a slice of bread. "They've asked me to stay out of the streets for a few more days. I don't really know why. Unless they're not yet ready to unleash me upon the astonished world."

He looked better. His hands no longer trembled. He seemed more confident. But then he would be, wouldn't he, if he was a spy and had got those dangerous hurdles of first meetings with the relatives safely over? He would start to relax a little.

She sat on the high kitchen stool and watched him as he made two uneven doorstep sandwiches crammed with ham. He handed her one.

"Sorry, no mustard," he said, smiling.

"That's all right. I don't like mustard."

"No more you do. Come into the other room and have a drink. Another present from downstairs. I've persuaded them gin won't overstimulate me."

Julie went into the other room and ate her sandwich and drank her gin and talked to the brother who might not be her brother. She had thought it would be easy. She had thought she had only to come back and take one good look at him and she would know, beyond all doubt. What she had not bargained for were the doubts already implanted in her mind. She found herself looking at him and thinking: *You've learned to talk like him very well, but, no, the way you move is not right.* She wanted to say to him: Walk across the room so that I can judge again. And when he did, fortuitously, to fetch an ashtray, she could not tell any longer if that was how Richard had always walked across a room or not.

She had so little to go on. She tried to summon up memories of him as he had been before his imprisonment and came up at once against the barrier of those vital ten years' difference in age. Sixteen when she was six, twenty when she was ten—they were a childhood apart. They had not played together as children or gone to school together or had at any time led parallel lives. They had had no long period of living in the same house, day after day, in each other's pockets, doing the same things, quarreling, fighting, sharing the same experiences, hating, enjoying, tolerating each other with that intensity of childhood that stamps the members of one family through like sticks of rock. They had never been forced by proximity to learn about each other in that stark, basic way which admits of no illusions, and which means in later life that however cleverly one may deceive the world, few brothers and sisters deceive each other.

All the recollections Julie held clearest in her mind were nothing more than snapshots: Richard playing cricket on a beach, Richard taking her on the walk to the church that summer of the flies, Richard teasing her at his wedding, Richard taking her to lunch on her birthday a few months before he vanished. That was little enough, but then she discovered something else. To have the memory of someone in your mind was one thing; to have the person before you at the same time confused not clarified the picture because the way the flesh and blood man moved, talked, laughed, merged into the memory until it was impossible to distinguish between them. Was the shape of this man's face the same as Richard's at his wedding, for example? Was the way the bones were set, the hollow of his eyes, the jawline—

"I'm quite real," he said.

It was like a cold finger against her neck. He had been sitting at ease, ankle resting on the other knee, and that indeed was a familiar pose of Richard's. He had been talking and smiling and watching her just as she watched him. His mental reactions seemed sharp and aware. Would his state of mind have improved so quickly if the distress she had witnessed on his first visit had been real?

She said, "I can't get over how much better you look today."

"Yes," he said. "I'm feeling better. I'm like an animal—

when I'm not well, I like to be in my own cave. I can rest here."

"Dorothy said you'd lost some teeth."

"Dorothy exaggerates. I wasn't feeling too good when she descended on me. I told her I had a toothache to get rid of her."

"But you should go to a dentist anyway," she said, "to check up."

He shrugged. "One day."

"Mr. Jenkins retired, you know. You'll have to go to another man." She did not look at him as she said it. She waited for him to ask why Jenkins should have retired at the tender age of thirty-eight, but he said nothing. She wanted to shake him to make him respond to all the awkward traps she laid for him. To make the right reply. She wanted to say: Convince me, Richard, please convince me. You are yourself, aren't you?

If all else fails, she had told herself, you rely on instinct, but it was instinct that failed her now. She waited for that flash of perception, that instinctive knowledge of him that would put the question beyond all possible doubt, but it did not come. She was frightened, and the fear confused her.

Richard leaned forward. "What is the matter, Julie?"

"I was thinking," she said, "of that cottage we had in the Wye Valley, of that time you took me for a long walk. Do you remember it? We ended up at a church I was about nine."

"It's strange what one remembers about childhood," he replied. "I remember telling Father, not long before he died, about some incident—the time I got my first fishing rod, something like that, vitally important to me, a red-letter day. We'd spent the whole day together. I'd remembered it all my life. But he'd completely forgotten it. To him it had been just another day."

He looked steadily at her as he spoke, and she raised her head and met his glance and saw the expression in his eyes. She read her own suspicion reflected in his eyes, and she felt a deeper stab of fear. She thought: *He's guessed.* And there went through her that tingling physical shock that electrifies you when someone finds you out in a lie. It was a sensation she had not had since childhood, and with it came the insidious thought: *You would not be afraid of your own brother.*

It was her silence in that moment that she regretted so bitterly later on. She was to wonder again and again if it would have made any difference if she had spoken. But she did not speak because she would not let herself accept the situation completely. She would not accept herself as unable to identify a person who should have been close to her and was not, whose experience and life and illness had created a barrier between them that she could not surmount. The doubts and uncertainties remained unresolved. She left him with no decision made.

She met Stephen in a pub. He silently fetched her a drink and waited until she was ready to speak.

"I don't know," she said.

"Blood didn't call to blood?"

"Please, don't make fun of me."

"Oh, my dear, believe me, I'm not making fun."

"It should, though, shouldn't it? You're right. I did believe that blood would call to blood."

"Not necessarily."

"You were certain from the beginning that it wasn't Richard."

"I'm glad you're out of there, anyway."

"If only Dorothy wasn't such an idiot," Julie said, "I'd make her go and see him. It needs someone who knows Richard well, an old friend, but someone calm and reasonable, someone we could trust, who'd make a cool judgment. I've become overemotional about it. Now I'm away from him I'm sure it must be Richard."

"I don't think we've got time for anyone else to see him. Don't forget those postcards, Julie. If that man is a substitute, then Richard is in desperate need of help."

"I know, I know." She put her head in her hands.

"Is your passport valid?"

"Yes."

"Do you know where it is?"

The question made her smile. She drew her hands apart and looked at him. "Yes, as it happens, I do. You know me very well, don't you?"

"Not as well as I hope to," he remarked. "I'll get us another drink."

She thought afterward it must have been the blond barmaid who served him who gave her the idea. It took some minutes to surface, however, while Stephen bought the drinks and carried them back to their table, while she asked him if he thought they should tell David Holbrook what was happening.

"Yes, perhaps we should tell someone," Stephen said. "Do you know how to get hold of him?"

"No . . . unless I asked at the flat below Richard's."

"I think we should avoid that house for the moment."

"There's a telephone number Dorothy has. They gave it to her for emergencies when Richard was arrested. I think we could reach Holbrook through that, or someone in his department anyway."

"On second thought," Stephen said, "I don't think we should tell anyone anything until we've been to France. We don't know who is who. I think it very unwise to trust anyone. We don't want to talk to the wrong man."

"I feel I'm in the middle of a spider's web," she said. "Everywhere you turn, sticky threads are waiting to trap you."

"A bit elaborate, but I know what you mean."

"Or as if everyone is wearing masks. You can only guess at the face underneath."

"Drink your drink like a good girl," Stephen said. "We've got a lot to do."

The barmaid came over and emptied the ashtrays. She smiled at them and made a remark about the weather.

"She fancies you," Julie observed when she had moved on.

"I fancy her," Stephen said. "I like big blondes."

The thought surfaced in Julie's mind and she said: "Michael."

"Michael?"

"Michael Brent. He's art editor for a publisher. I've done some work for him. He was at college with Richard. He'd go and see him. He knows he's back. I told him in confidence. And he's a very shrewd man."

Stephen paused before replying. She could tell he was wondering how important it was to her.

"We haven't got time," he said at last. "I want to be off first thing in the morning."

"He could go today."

"Wouldn't your brother be rather surprised to see him?"

"He knows I've worked for Michael. I mentioned it the other day, when I first saw him. It would be some sort of confirmation, whatever opinion Mike got of him."

"Can you get hold of him?"

"I know his telephone number. At least I've got it at the flat."

Stephen drained the last of his drink and put the empty glass down carefully.

"How many other people have you told in confidence about Richard's return?"

"None." She added, "It's nice of you to be jealous, but there's no need."

He smiled. "Surprisingly, I wasn't thinking about that. I was wondering how much time we've got before the news leaks out. We want the right Richard Davidge before the cameras and giving the interviews."

"Perhaps David Holbrook and his superiors wouldn't mind about that. If they allow the wrong one to be interviewed, the other side will think they've won, won't they? Then we slip the right one in his place, and we've got a double agent of our own. The real one will be able to pass back any information we like, and they'll accept every planted word in good faith."

"My God!" he said. "I didn't know it ran in families. Are you sure you're not a spy, too?"

"It's quite a clever idea, isn't it?"

"Brilliant. But you realize what it means? You have made up your mind about the identity of the man after all."

She looked down at the table and slowly traced a pattern on the plastic top with a wandering finger.

"No," she said. "Because I don't believe any of it. These ideas, these suppositions, they're like a game. None of it seems real to me. Seeing Richard again this morning, even he no longer seemed real. But Michael's mind would be clean; he wouldn't be encumbered by all this—" She moved her hands in a helpless gesture. "He might come back and say yes or no, and we'd know."

"Would you condemn the man in the flat on another's word?"

"What do you mean?"

"Well, what do you imagine his fate is going to be if he is a substitute? Suppose Michael said no, that's not him, and we told Holbrook, and he had the same brilliant idea of using him as you had. What do you think they'll do with him next? They can't put him on trial. He'll be a secret that has to say secret. He'll have to disappear completely."

"You mean they might kill him," she said flatly. "But I wouldn't tell anyone on Michael's word. It might help me to make up my own mind, that's all. I know you're right; we can't say a word to anyone in authority until we know whether Richard is in St.-Malo. You're so sure, Stephen, but it's not as easy for me."

He shook his head. "No, I'm not sure. I've never been involved in anything remotely like this before, and I'm not sure of anything except the need to find out the truth."

Their voices were quiet and matter-of-fact. To anyone watching, they might have been discussing train times. They were blending in with their surroundings in what she realized was probably an intentional way as far as Stephen was concerned. The orange shaded lights glowing dimly in the renovated, lowered ceiling; the interminable, droning background music, like waves of lukewarm custard, that never reached a satisfying dominant chord: the muted tweed upholstery; the muted patterned carpet of orange and brown and plain dead beige, were all intended to soothe, quiet, nullify. It was not a place for good cheer. Anyone getting drunk in this bar wouldn't sing for joy; he'd be sick in the corner. *It isn't really a proper pub,* Julie thought. She didn't like it. She liked engraved mirrors and brass and no tarting-up.

"All right," Stephen said. "Ring up your friend Michael and ask him to meet us somewhere about six. I'll be back by then."

Alarm seized her. "Where are you going?"

"I've got things to arrange, tickets and so on. Now go home, ring your friend, find your passport, pack your bag, and wait."

"What about money?"

"I've got enough money. We'll sort that out later. And when you get home," he said, as he put her in a taxi, "stay put."

At the third try, Julie got hold of Michael. He was surprised but obliging. It was obvious that at first he thought she was ringing about the illustration she had left for him. When he realized it had to do with Richard, his interest increased. She could tell she had aroused his curiosity by the way he listened. An air of sharp attention came over the wires. As always, getting a little flustered when she had to prevaricate, she said only that she and a friend of Richard's wanted to talk to him about Richard.

"I'll be waiting," he said. "But I can't stay terribly long. I have to meet someone."

"Oh . . . "

"Does that matter? Do you want me to put them off?"

"No, of course not. Well, we'll see you later then, Mike. Good-bye."

"Good-bye, Julie."

In between the calls, Julie followed her other instructions. She found her passport and packed a grip and waited. She found the waiting enlivened by the necessity of solving various domestic problems. What was she to do, for instance, about the milk and the papers? She would prefer no one to know what she was up to, but if she said nothing then the milk would stack up and papers accumulate and people would begin to wonder if she was dead in her bed or, at the very least, they would correctly assume she had gone away. But if she left notes canceling her orders, they would know for certain she was away. It was extraordinary how impossible it was to lead a completely detached life. Whatever you did, you always left a thread trailing behind you. But what was more extraordinary was that she found herself worrying about, of all people, Miss Dawson. If Julie simply vanished without a word for an indefinite number of days, Miss Dawson, she felt instinctively, was going to become anxious. She might even, after the business with Robinson, call the police. In the end she wrote a note to Miss Dawson and put it through her door, saying she had been called away on a working trip and could they use her milk and collect and keep her papers? There wasn't much she could do about her post. Mr. Morfitt would automatically keep it. But there were often days when there was nothing for her, so he wouldn't immediately think she was away, and after this morning he would be in no mood to seek her out.

Stephen came back at five.

"I hope your alarm clock works," he said. "I want us to be on the first boat we can make."

"I never asked you," she said. "How do we get to St.-Malo?"

"There are various ways, by ship and by plane, most of which don't appear to be functioning on a Sunday in April, but I thought the simplest way would be to cross the Channel and drive down. It has the added purpose of confusing the trail if anyone follows us."

"I haven't got a car," Julie said. "Have you?"

"Not here. That's what I've spent most of the afternoon arranging. I've been on the phone to a friend of mine in

Dieppe. He's going to see there's a rented car waiting for us, one we can leave anywhere we like."

"Even when I'm going on holiday," she said, "I get sick with apprehension. But this . . . "

"Put on a glamorous dress," he said, "something that shows off your legs, and I'll stun you with food and wine."

"All right. But you sit right there and don't leave the flat. I'm getting frightened again." She tried to smile. "I keep asking myself what are we doing, we two against these international spy rings."

"I don't know," Stephen said, "I'm just beginning to enjoy myself. This is the one simple part, getting from A to B, that I think even we two can manage. Are you the kind of girl who needs seasick pills?"

She turned from the bedroom door. "Yes," she said, "I am."

"I thought you might be. I bought you some."

She paused, and then she said, echoing one of the first things he had ever said to her, "Are you always going to look after me like this?"

"Yes," he said. "I believe I am."

Michael was waiting for them in the foyer of his club, a small, comfortable, slightly shabby establishment with the atmosphere of a well-lived-in country house and a membership consisting largely of professional artists, writers, and actors. He looked as relaxed as he ever managed to be sitting in an armchair reading the evening paper.

As soon as she saw him, Julie got cold feet.

"I've changed my mind," she murmured to Stephen as they approached him. "Don't say anything."

Stephen raised an inquiring eyebrow.

"I suddenly feel it's wrong to bring him into it."

It was an instinctive reaction, perhaps triggered off by this unexpectedly domestic-looking aspect of Michael. The dropping of the social mask has the tendency either to age or make younger. Michael, content with his own company, looked younger. He had the unself-conscious, slightly vulnerable air that people often acquire when alone and unaware that they are being observed. It made Julie see with unusual clarity that in this affair he was placed on one side of the fence and she and Stephen on the other. Michael had the innocence of the uninvolved. She felt then the weight of the burden of responsibility those three pretty picture postcards had placed on her shoulders. She could never be detached again. Unconsciously, her hand sought Stephen's for the reassurance that she was not alone. He gripped her hand gently in response and let it go.

Michael stood up to greet them. He kissed Julie and shook hands with Stephen.

"I hope you didn't mind trailing over here," he said, "but I've two Americans meeting me here in half an hour, so it seemed the simplest arrangement."

So he could not, in any case, have seen Richard before she and Stephen left for France. She was mildly relieved to know that.

Michael gathered other chairs around the table and ordered drinks. After a few minutes of generalities, he leaned forward and asked Julie, "How is Richard?" He glanced at Stephen. "I gathered you wanted to talk to me about him."

"I'm sorry, Michael," Julie said. "I've really got you to meet us on false pretenses. I was worried about Richard when I rang you. He had seemed so ill and strange when I saw him, and you being an old friend and Dorothy so silly—"

"Ah—" Michael smiled. He said to Stephen, "Have you met Dorothy Davidge?"

"Once."

"Once is usually enough." He turned back to Julie. "As an old friend, you wanted me to go and cheer him up, is that it?"

"Well, that was the idea. But it doesn't matter now. It's unimportant. I've spoken to him again, and I'm quite happy about him now. I'm sorry for disturbing your evening."

She had told Stephen that Michael was a shrewd man; now she rather wished it wasn't true. His brown eyes were sharply observant. But he made no comment.

"I'm always happy to see you, Julie." He said to Stephen, "Apart from being beautiful, she's a talented girl."

Stephen smiled across at her. "So I'm learning."

And then Michael began to probe. His curiosity, once aroused, Julie realized, was not so easily satisfied.

"Have you seen Richard?" he asked Stephen.

"No, not since he got back."

"I shared digs with him for a while."

"Yes, so Julie said."

"He's a very interesting character." He made the remark slowly with an emphasis that invited comment or speculation. In reply, Stephen turned the conversation back to him.

"Did you ever imagine he would become a spy?"

Michael shrugged. "Looking back on it, I'm not really surprised." He added: "It would be interesting to see him again. I wonder if he remembers me."

"Yes, of course he does," Julie said. "And he knows I've been working for you. I told him."

"Where's he living?"

"His old flat." She could not prevent herself from saying, since it was so much in the forefront of her mind, "He's very changed. In physical appearance, I mean."

But Michael seemed to attach no significance to it. "It's not surprising. It's hardly safe to move about at all, is it? It's getting so one's afraid to cross to France even for fear of committing *lèse majesté*. Of course, the French prefer despotism. They feel it more natural to indulge in occasional revolutions than to exercise continual responsible rule. Julie doesn't believe me when I tell her democracy is dying. We are ruled by faceless bureaucrats and lecherous puritans."

Julie laughed. "That's an impossible combination."

"It's not." He grinned at her. "You think about it. 'All right for me but not for you' is their philosophy."

"I've met them," Stephen agreed. "They're endemic in every society. We have no monopoly on them."

Michael asked him about his work, and Stephen told them an immensely long and involved and funny story about an exhibition in Bulgaria. The two men liked each other. How much Mike enjoyed life, Julie thought, and how infectious such enjoyment was. How simple, how pleasant it was to sit with two friends and talk, and with the awareness that impresses such a moment on the mind, she observed the details of the room, the decorative plaster work, the charming eighteenth-century fireplace. She saw two men standing in the doorway, looking around. The shape of their heads, the way their hair was cut, the material of their suits stamped them immediately and unmistakably as American.

"Your friends are here," she said.

She and Stephen got up to go. As Michael said good-bye to her, he added quietly, "I'm glad I've met him, though I'm sorry to lose the prospect of our middle-aged affair."

"Is it so obvious?" she said.

"Obvious," he said kindly, "but mutual."

She laughed and kissed him again.

They returned to the flat about midnight, warmed through

with wine and each other's company. They drank coffee together and talked and smiled rather foolishly and fell silent, looking in silence at each other across the small space of the room.

"It's after one," Stephen said. "I should go. We've got an early start."

"Yes," she said. "Where are you staying?"

He told her. "That's something else I did during my busy afternoon, booked myself a room."

He stood up and Julie stood up, and he kissed her for quite a long time and said good-night and said he would collect her in the morning.

She said yes and followed him into the hall. He picked up his bag and his raincoat, while she watched him in silence, and opened the flat door. Then he shut the door and put down bag and raincoat and said, "This is ridiculous," and took her in his arms.

"Ridiculous," she agreed.

"After all," he murmured against her neck, "they're bound to have given me up and let the room."

"Bound to," Julie said.

"You never can," he said, "rely on hotels."

Early in the morning she was awakened by the first creeping strands of day and by the unaccustomed feel of another body in her bed. She saw the pile of clothes, hers flung untidily on a chair, trailing on the floor, one shoe on its sole, one sideways, and on the other side of the room his suit hanging on the wardrobe and his shirt on one of her hangers. It pleased her very much. It seemed exactly right. She drew her arm across her face and touched the skin with her tongue. She tasted of him, and when she stretched, her feet entwined with his. She turned on her side to study his sleeping face and fell asleep herself, still smiling.

Chapter 5

~~~~~~

The surge and rush and push of the boisterous wind pinned her against the rail. It seized her hair and flung it about her face and curled it into sea-salt tendrils. It filled her eyes with her own salt tears and filled her mind with such exhilaration that she flung her arms around Stephen and shouted into the wind, "Isn't it marvelous! Isn't it wonderful!"

The sky was a pale cerulean blue streaked with wild horse-tails, and the sea swelled and moved like the rippling muscled back of some enormous animal. As the ship's bow dipped, the spray was caught and tossed upward against her face so that soon her cheeks became covered with a fine sprinkling of salt.

Leaving London, leaving England, leaving the doubts and the problems was like running from a dark cave into sunlight. All confusion dropped away, left behind like unimportant debris in the wake of the ship.

Below, where they had been for a drink, the throb and oil smell of the engines had begun to have its old familiar lurching, sickening effect, but up here she felt only excitement.

"Better?" Stephen cried.

"Oh, yes, yes!"

Standing behind her at the rail, he put his arms around her waist and hugged her to him and bent his head and kissed her cheek.

"You taste of salt," he said.

The boat was half empty, which gave its passengers the feeling of being elite, as if the passage had been arranged solely for them. The crew, under no pressure, were relaxed and smiling, and a pleasant conspiracy seemed to exist among them all that they were all on a holiday.

"It's a good thing to come back to the sea," Julie said. "You forget about it in cities. The sea . . . it's a word that goes on forever, limitless."

" 'Fair stood the wind for France,' " he quoted, " 'when we our sails advanced,' making for—Dieppe."

"That's what I mean," Julie said. "It's elemental and historical."

"Not to mention," he said, "poetical and nautical."

She laughed and turned in his arms so that she could look up into his eyes. Dark gray eyes with dark lashes flecked with salt, eyes that were amused by her and smiled at her.

"How is your French?" she asked.

"Impeccable. How's yours?"

"Superb. The only trouble is no one in France ever understands a word I say."

He laughed and kissed her. They stood lip to lip. She said, "When you do that I get quite weak."

"I get quite weak myself. Ah"—he threw back his head—"breathe that restorative air! Do you know your hands are frozen? Let's go and have something to eat."

They had left at an early hour that seemed to Julie already too late, and driven in a lonely taxi down deserted Sunday streets. She had never thought they would manage to catch the train, but they had.

And once in the train, that detached excitement that accompanied every journey took hold of her. To go from London by train in the early morning was to slip away in secrecy. The rumpled backsides of city streets and tenements, the weed-stricken, straggling grass banks of the suburban stretches, the grazing horses in the lonely field, the pools and sandy tracks and uncut hedges, the gravel and smoke and abandoned cars. It was the other, the neglected, the uncared-for side of the façade you saw through the train window, like the unpainted side of a stage set. It was the traveler on the roads who saw the intended face, the neat flower beds and painted doors, the shop fronts rather than the warehouses. And there was nothing to match the steep fall between the downs, crowded with their marching lines of houses, to the first prospect of the Channel, the beginning of adventure. Because her physical senses were aroused, every emotion was heightened, every small incident held an unusual and particular significance. She was happy and knew it, and knew it could never be repeated—never in quite the same way.

When they left the boat at Dieppe, Stephen walked her to a café off the Grande Rue, near the church of St. Jacques. They sat with their thick cups of morning coffee by the quiet square, and Julie forgot for long moments why they were there and what they had come to do. After a while, Stephen looked at his watch and went to telephone. When he came back, he said, "It's all fixed. I'm going to collect the car."

"I'll come with you." She began to rise.

"No. Stay here. I shan't be long."

She did not like to be left, but she waited as patiently as she could. A bell began to sound, tolling monotonously with the thin, slightly tinny timbre that is to English ears so characteristic of continental bells. There was a smell of newly baked bread and a faint memory in the air of the sluiced-down slabs of the fish market, and the passersby on their way to or from church all seemed to be dressed in black. Behind her the proprietor poured himself a cognac and settled down to read yesterday's paper.

A shadow fell on her. For the split second before she looked up and saw Stephen, she knew alarm. "Are you ready?" he said. "We should get going."

A black Peugeot was parked in the empty square. Stephen tossed their bags and coats in the back. Julie went around and got in the passenger seat. Stephen took off his jacket and flung that in the back, too. He got in beside her.

"Comfortable?" he said.

"Yes, very." She smiled at him. "I hope you know the way."

"Vaguely," he said. "Very vaguely." He also, it seemed, could not escape the feeling of holiday. He pulled out some maps and spent a few minutes sorting through them. Finally, he folded one back into a neat rectangle and handed it to Julie. "There you are. You be navigator. First stop Rouen."

Of all her memories of that strange time, their flight through the sunlit April of France was to be the happiest. In reality it was not so carefree; it was full of small fears and apprehensions and underlying hints of trouble to come, but in retrospect it became one glorious rush of speed and excitement through a green abundant countryside ripe with spring.

Stephen drove very fast. It was some time before Julie realized he was seriously concerned that they might have been followed from England, and be now leading Richard's enemies to him.

"Keep an eye out," he asked her, "for any car that stays with us longer than twenty miles."

She looked out at the apple orchards and the gently rising hills and then back through the rear window at the road behind them.

"There's nothing behind at all at the moment."

He nodded. "Good. It would be nice if it stayed that way."

At Rouen, they drove in sparse traffic straight through the center of the city without stopping, and crossed the Seine. On the other side of the bridge, Julie had several moments of confusion before she guided them through the suburbs on to the road to Pont-Audemer.

"You're very good," Stephen assured her.

"I'm not navigating," she said. "I'm reading signposts, and I don't know if it's significant or not, but a car followed us through all those diversions and is still behind us."

Stephen glanced into the mirror. "What's it like?"

"It's a big gray car, French number plates, the driver is a man, no passengers."

Stephen slowed down until they were merely ambling along, and soon, when the road ahead was clear, the gray car passed them and drove on fast, leaving them behind. After five miles, there was still no sign of it.

Stephen smiled at her. "False alarm."

They were on their way to Caen, through the thick wooded Norman countryside when the green car picked them up. If she had not been by now intensely aware of everything that moved in the road behind them, Julie might have missed it. It stayed at such a discreet distance, keeping two or three cars, or a lorry, between them, rarely in sight, except where possibilities arose of the Peugeot branching away on another route.

By the time they had passed Pont-l'Evêque they were sure. Stephen had varied his speed, and the green car had stayed at the same distance. He had pulled up by the side of the road and smoked a cigarette, letting it pass. When they drove on, they passed it themselves at a gas station; a few minutes later it was back in position behind them.

"This isn't coincidence," Stephen remarked.

"What shall we do?" Julie said.

"Well, I haven't much experience of this sort of thing. They're obviously experts. We're not going to lose them on this road."

"Did you see how many there were?"

"Two, I think."

Julie said nervously, "What do you suppose they intend to do?"

"Nothing. Just keep us in sight. It's your brother they're after, not us. I think we'll try to lose them in Caen. If they keep with us beyond that, they'll know we're going to Brittany. But if we get away from them in Caen we could be going to Cherbourg, doubling back to Le Havre, going south to Alençon and Tours, or even the long way around to Paris. They won't know. They'll have to try all the routes."

"And how are we going to lose them in Caen?"

"I don't know. I think I'll have to drive like a maniac and hope the police don't stop me."

Julie did not pause to consider at that moment the fact that the green car had provided her by its very presence with a final piece of evidence concerning the identity of the man in St.-Malo. She was simply caught up in the nervous tension of the pursuit.

Stephen had begun slowing down. "There's a *routiers* ahead. If it's open, let's eat. We can afford to stop now. Later, we might not get the opportunity."

The restaurant was open. They sat with the lorry drivers and ate enormous helpings of rich casseroled beef, redolent with herbs and wine and thick and brown with its long hours of cooking. Julie found she was ravenously hungry, and so apparently was Stephen. They ate in a companionable but concentrated silence. Stephen tore his bread in half and mopped up the last traces of the juices on his place. It had been a long time since that coffee in Dieppe.

He smiled at her. "That ought to give us the strength to beat the bandits."

She had been admiring what she supposed might be called his coolness and thought how right she had been to have dubbed him the man to be with in an emergency. How completely and utterly useless she would have been by herself in such a situation. What would she have done, she wondered, if those postcards had come to her alone, if there had been no Stephen to talk to, to work out the implications and the dangers, to get her so quickly and efficiently on her way to Brittany? Who would she have turned to? She found her own answer was immediate and in its way surprising. She would have gone to Michael. It was a strange reaction because her instinct the previous evening to keep Michael out of it had been so strong. And she still had that feeling. It was dangerous to be involved in this complex tangle, and she did not want Michael in danger, but if she had been alone, she would have run to him. He had been right when he had said they were friends.

Shephen was offering her a cigarette. "You look very pensive."

She took the cigarette, bending her head to his lighter. "I was thinking about Michael."

"Ah—I'm sorry to hear that."

She looked at him in mild exasperation. "Now, why?"

"Because he's a man with a lot of charm, and he's in love with you."

"No, he's not. He just says that, as they say, to all the girls."

"He may fool you, but he doesn't me. If he put his mind to it, he could be a dangerous rival."

She couldn't tell if he was joking or not.

"He's a friend," she protested.

"There's no such thing as friendship between a man and a woman. At least," he amended, "not friendship alone. Even in the most platonic of relationships there's that element 'if only' or 'perhaps, one day.' "

One day, when we're old and gray, Michael had said.

"That's why I'm sorry you're thinking about him," Stephen said. "It makes me disturbingly jealous." He stubbed his cigarette out and stood up, calling for the bill, pulling out a crumpled handful of notes to pay it. His expression was preoccupied, but whether with her or with the green car waiting for them somewhere out on the road, she could not tell. "Come on," he said. "On with the chase." From the grasp of his hand, she knew he had been joking in nothing he had said.

On the outskirts of Caen, Stephen pulled the car to the side of the road and switched off the engine. The silence and stillness were a relief. Julie turned and looked behind them. "There's no sign of them."

"They'll be there somewhere. Let's have a look at the map."

He studied the routes radiating from the boundary roads of the city carefully.

"I've driven through here once before," he said. "I vaguely remember it."

"We don't have to go into the center at all," Julie pointed out. "See." She traced it with her finger. "We can go right around and pick up the N 175 here."

"Yes. But we're not going to do that. That would make it too clear."

She glanced back once again. "Do you really think they're still with us? I haven't seen them for miles. Perhaps it was a coincidence, after all."

"They're still with us," Stephen said.

Something about him disturbed her. Some undertone, some undercurrent. She could not pin down the source of her unease, unless it was that quality she had first recognized in him, his detachment, his efficiency. *I don't know him at all,* she thought. *I know everything and nothing about him.* She felt isolated, sitting so close to him. She put her hand out and took his hand, wanting to feel his flesh, wanting the warmth and friendship of a clasped hand. With a gesture of absentminded affection, he raised her hand to his lips and kissed it.

When he spoke, she realized he was not at all detached. His eyes had the excitement of the race in them; his voice was eager. "Shall we risk it?" he said.

She had not heard what he had said before.

"Yes," she said. "Let's risk it."

He started the car up and began to drive, not too fast, well within any limit of safety. They came to a roundabout, a large circular junction of six roads.

"Place de la Demi-Lune," Julie read from the map. "That's a romantic name."

He approached it slowly. "They'll have to come up closer to see us here. They've got to know which road we take."

She was turned right around in her seat, an arm across the back of it, staring through the rear window. She saw a flash of green.

"There they are! Stephen, they're coming up!"

He put his foot down and roared flat out down the Rue d'Auge, heading for the center of the city.

Caen, in Julie's blurred impression, took the shape of a

wheel, with the straight streets like spokes running to the green hub of the castle hill. It was a confused, rushed impression, taken on the wing, of an ancient city built of modern buildings, the flat façades biscuit-colored in the afternoon light, wide glass shop fronts fleeing past the car window, an industrial city swelling around medieval churches, a city smashed flat and rebuilt and still bearing, after twenty years, the slightly shiny air of a burned face smoothed over with grafted skin.

They reached the castle mound, and Stephen slowed the car as they began to circle it. At this moment the green car was quite out of sight.

"This is it," Stephen said.

He asked Julie to look out for a possible turning to the left, so that they could cut through back streets to their exit road without going along the obvious route. She looked at the map, saw a street that would do, looked up, saw the street immediately to her left, on the wall, and cried out, "Here, turn here!"

He swung left and accelerated. She saw a car approaching them on their side of the road. The driver swerved, yelling. "One way," she shouted. "Stephen, it's one way!"

He nodded, frowning. The street ahead was empty. He went faster, sweeping up the length of it. The first turning off went right. He took it, then went left, and right again, winding around the twists of narrow streets. They passed a church and found themselves on a broad road; then they were at a fork. "Which way, which way?"

She caught sight of a street plaque, CAPONIERE. "Left, left!" They were away down it. There was nothing behind them. They went on and on, Julie looking back, eyes straining; nothing. They were on the outskirts. They passed a signpost. She sighed with relief to find they were on the right road. They left Caen behind.

"We've done it," Stephen said. He put a hand on her thigh. "We've done it, darling!" He was exhilarated.

She leaned back. She smiled at him. "I'm surprised we haven't got half the police force in Caen after us."

"We would have if it hadn't been Sunday. That was a brilliant idea of yours to take us up a one-way street the wrong way."

"I'm sorry—"

"No, I mean it. That was what finally lost them. They've

probably assumed we went right around and north. They would see quite clearly we weren't on the road out to Avranches." He handed her his cigarettes. "Light me one, will you? Well," he said, "halfway to St.-Malo." He smiled. "I enjoyed that."

The rest of the journey was uneventful. They drove on and on, through the villages and the war-battered towns, all rebuilt with the same blond stone that made them look alike. The noise of the engine soothed her, and the countryside, like the English countryside, green, flowering, beautiful. She dozed, forgetting again as she had in Dieppe, why they were there, what they were doing. The journey became not an interlude, but an end in itself.

At Avranches, Stephen stopped for a drink. She asked if he was tired. He shook his head. He seemed relaxed. He said he liked driving. When they had finished the drink, he suggested they eat something. They had an omelette. When they moved, she felt stiff. London and Richard seemed in another life. She seemed to have always been driving with Stephen.

"We shall pass Mont-St.-Michel," he said.

The light was changing. They could smell the sea. A mist was rising, far out. They drove down the escarpment to sea level. Far away, sinister, swathed in mist, she saw the turreted island.

"It doesn't look real."

"No." He drove more slowly now.

It was past nine o'clock when they reached St.-Malo. It was raining, solid walls of warm rain. Julie found it hard to see. They drove along the sea front and came to the walled town. He parked the car outside. "We'd better leave the car here till we find a hotel. The streets inside are narrow and one-way. You wait here."

"No, I'm coming."

"You'll get drenched."

"So will you."

As they walked through the gateway, the rain eased. "It's a good omen."

The hotel room they found was on the third floor with a window from which she could glimpse the sea beyond the ramparts. They had not been asked if they wanted one room or two. It had been taken for granted they would have one. There was space in a courtyard for the car. They fetched the car, had the bags carried up, and shut the door. On the boat they had bought a bottle of brandy. Stephen poured out two measures and handed Julie one. She sipped it slowly.

"I like being enclosed in walls," she said. "I feel safe."

Stephen had collapsed on the bed, flat out, his eyes closed. He caught her wrist as she passed and pulled her down to him, enclosing her in his arms.

"You're tired."

"Yes." He opened his eyes. "We can't look for Richard to-night. He won't expect us at night. He'll wait for us in day-light. Let's have tonight to ourselves. This one night." His voice was low and urgent.

She thought, *Is it to end so soon?* She held him close to her, and for the first hour, he slept.

Next morning the rain had cleared away. The sky was the joyous blue of a Renaissance painting. The sea was a shim-mering sweep of water in a romantically beautiful bay. Din-ard and the black broken coast of the Breton bays beyond were as clearly delineated as the roofs below their window. The breath of the sea was sweet.

They ate their *petit déjeuner* in the small tiled bar of the hotel as the maid sorted linen in the hall outside. The win-dows of the bar were hung with thick yellow lace curtains and the tabletops of the round iron tables were marble.

Stephen took out of his pocket the postcard of St.-Malo that had been sent to him and laid it on the table. They sat looking at it in silence.

"You think he'll wait there, somewhere on those ramparts," Julie said at last.

"Yes. All we've got to do is walk along the walls and we'll find him." Stephen sounded completely confident, as if there were no doubts; but then he had never had any doubts.

Julie felt breathless with apprehension. "Stephen, I can't bear the suspense. Let's go."

"It's early."

"Never mind. Please let's go."

"All right." He stood up, his chair scraping on the floor.

There was a door from the bar leading directly on to the street. He closed it behind them and they began to walk toward the shadow of the wall.

The ramparts of St.-Malo enclose it completely. From the Grande Porte on the Quai St.-Vincent, past the yacht basin and the quay where the steamers for Jersey wait, past the thin length of the Môles des Noires, where the wind is never still, along the beaches where the children search for shrimp in the hollows of the rocks when the long tides fall back beyond the islands, buttressed by small towers and forts, flanked by the square gray castle from which it curves back to its beginning, the wall secures a citadel of tall houses and narrow streets, of miniature *places* and bustling markets, an enclave used by pirates as their homing nest and still so defensible that during the Second World War the Germans held out for weeks before abandoning it to burning ruin.

If she had been a fugitive, Julie thought, she would have felt safe here, hidden by the walls, with the warren of streets and alleys to dart and run before pursuit and the sea at your back to escape to. Seen from the height of the ramparts, the fire which had destroyed the pirate city seemed to have left little trace. The rebuilt eighteenth-century houses, reconstructed so perfectly by a loving imagination, were serene and peaceful in the clear light, the windows gleaming with mother-of-pearl reflections from the sea. In the bay, two fishing boats heading out on the morning tide cut across the surface of the sea like scissors cutting gray cloth.

"He's not here," Julie said.

They had climbed the steps to the top of the wall and walked along the broad pathway until they were, as far as they could judge, on the exact section of the ramparts photographed for the colored postcard. In either direction there was no one to be seen but a woman with a small child and an old man sitting reading a newspaper.

"We're too early," Stephen said.

"What time would you expect him to come?" She added: "If he is here."

"I don't know. A little later." He glanced at his watch. "Between eleven and twelve."

She was impressed by his conviction. "Is that when you'd come if you were he?"

He shrugged. "It seems a reasonable time."

"Perhaps he doesn't expect us yet."

"He would expect you to come at once, wouldn't he?" he asked her.

She nodded. "Yes. Yes, he would." She smiled. "Provided he could credit me with intelligence enough to work out his message."

"Well"—he smiled back—"he'd know you'd have me to help you."

He pulled out his cigarettes and lit one for her, and they leaned against the retaining wall, smoking and gazing out to sea.

Stephen waved a hand vaguely in the direction of one of the islands. "Chateaubriand is buried out there."

"That doesn't mean very much to me, I'm afraid. I've never read him. Though I've eaten his steak."

Stephen smiled, "Are we talking about the same man?"

Julie turned and stood with her back resting against the cool stone. The child had pulled away from her mother's hand and was running tipsily from side to side, her plump legs too fat and buttery to steer a straight course.

"I'm restless," Julie said. "I can't just wait here. Let's walk a bit."

"All right." He dropped his cigarette on the ground and put it out with one quick twist of his foot. "Let's do the grand tour. It's highly recommended."

They walked the circle of the ramparts until Julie began to grow confused as to where they were. There were few people about. In August, Stephen told her, the beaches would be packed, the streets with tourists and day-trippers from the Channel Islands, the souvenir shops bursting.

"I like it better as it is now," Julie said. "Living its own life. Everybody having a reason for being here. I like to be the only tourist."

"Except that you're not," he said. "You're here for a purpose, too."

Something in his voice made her look up. He was staring ahead, along the path. Suddenly she realized where they were. She recognized the place; the seat where the old man had read his paper, the path the child had run along, the particular angle of the view. They had walked right around the city and were back where they had begun. And leaning against the wall, gazing out to sea as they had done and in almost the very spot where they had stopped before, was a man. He was wearing slacks and a thick fisherman's sweater. His face was turned away from them. His shoulders were hunched as if he were cold or as if, Julie thought, he were braced against an attack.

"There he is," Stephen said.

She stood still. She felt an incredible nervousness and excitement. It seemed impossible that they had finally reached the culmination of their search; that the explanation painstakingly fitted together from odd clues and strange messages and instinct and logic, and gambled on in the rushed journey, should be proved true. All the questions solved, all the puzzles explained. She called softly, "Richard?"

He did not move. "He won't hear you," Stephen said. "We're too far away."

They walked nearer, Julie dragging a little at Stephen's arm. When they were within a few feet of him, Stephen said, "Hello, Davidge."

The man turned around. He turned quickly, in one movement, but for Julie, the emotional intensity of that moment, the suspense of anticipation, prolonged it, created an illusion of time hanging, of a vacuum in which he moved with the agonizing deliberation of slow motion. His body swayed, arms reluctantly leaving their resting place on the wall, shoulders coming around till his back was at last against the wall and he was facing them.

He was taller than she was, but not as tall as Stephen. What little she could see of his skin was tanned and weatherbeaten. He was wearing dark glasses that hid half his face. He had grown a beard. For Julie the test became not whether she recognized him, but whether he knew her.

He looked from one to the other of them. He said, "Julie," and put out his hand. He said, "Thank God," and then seemed for a long moment to be speechless.

"Well," Stephen said. "Your postcards worked, you see. Here we are, both of us."

Julie couldn't speak. She kept staring at her brother as if in a dream.

He suddenly laughed. "You don't recognize me in a beard. I didn't have much choice about growing it." He fingered the glasses. "But I've been hoping with that and the glasses my dearest relative couldn't recognize me, and it seems I'm right."

She thought of the man in England. It seemed ironic in view of the importance of his identity that Richard should have had to disguise himself so thoroughly.

She said, "How are you, Richard?"

He squeezed her hand. "All right."

"Does anyone know you're here?" Stephen said. "Has anyone been watching you?"

He looked puzzled, and then alarmed. "No. I don't think so."

Julie said, "We were followed to Caen. Stephen shook them off."

"Oh?" He turned quickly to Stephen. "So they got on to you. How? Did someone see the postcards?"

He did, Julie thought, *the other one. I showed him the postcard from Lyons. I asked if he remembered sending it.*

"They would watch Julie automatically," Stephen was saying. "There's nothing to worry about."

"Are you quite sure you got rid of them?" He gripped Stephen's sleeve. "There's no chance of them following you here?"

"It's highly unlikely, but I don't think we should be sure of anything. The sooner we can get you back to England, the better."

"How did you get here?" Julie said. "How have you been living?"

"It's a long and tedious story. It'll keep." He kept glancing beyond them, nervous, restless. She could feel the tension in him like a spring as she had in that first meeting with the other man in the Regent's Park flat. Both, the true and the false, were subject to the same pressures.

He took off the sunglasses and rubbed his eyes, and Julie saw in him glimpses of the Richard who used to be, the young Richard of her childhood, the face unformed and unmarked by experience.

"Let's go down to the beach," Stephen suggested. "We can talk there."

They walked along the hard sand by the water's edge, three visitors taking a morning walk for their health. Julie walked in the middle, the men talking across her. It was cold down on the shore. The fresh wind swept around the open bay into their faces. There was no protection from it.

"I've been here over a week," Richard was saying. "I hitchhiked across country from Lyons. I told them when I took the room I was recovering from an illness. I was very tired the first day I got here. I sent the postcard and waited."

"Why did you come here?" Julie asked. "Why didn't you go to a British official or the French police? Wouldn't they have helped you?"

"I don't particularly trust the French police or the intelligence of the average British official. I had no papers. I had no time. I couldn't afford to trust anyone. Even if they had been sympathetic, they would have taken time to check. It would have been too dangerous for me to wait for bureaucracy to ask questions. When you are a fugitive, you feel you are hunted, even if there is no one behind you. And they were looking for me. I knew that. As they still are, you tell me. I kept away from all my old contacts. After two years I wasn't sure what might have happened to them." He repeated, "I couldn't afford to trust anyone. There was only you, Julie, I dare trust."

He was still tired. His voice betrayed it, and the way he seemed with a kind of thankful relief to be handing over the burden of decision to Stephen. He had gone on long enough alone. Now he was with friends it seemed as if the last of his energy were slipping away from him. *He can't give up yet,* Julie thought. *He's not safe yet. He doesn't know what is waiting for him in England. When are we going to tell him?* She looked to Stephen for a lead. *I'm dependent on him, too,* she thought. *We would both of us be lost without him.*

As if he read her thought, Stephen said, "Why me?" Then she realized he was questioning Richard.

Richard shrugged. "I remembered you and how to reach you. Perhaps because you were the last person I spoke to in Lyons. I thought Julie would need someone to help her. I thought you might be the man."

"You have friends in Lyons?"

Richard looked at him inquiringly. Stephen explained. "Someone wrote the envelopes, bought the stamps, posted them."

"A girl in the pension wrote the addresses for me. I told her I'd sprained my hand. I posted them." He looked across at Stephen. "This is more than curiosity. This is the beginning of an inquisition. Why?"

"Why come here to St.-Malo?" Stephen said. "Why not Paris or a Channel port?"

"Because I thought it less likely to be watched. Because I thought it might be easier to leave. Because I remembered it." There was a snap to his voice, an aggressive edge. Julie wondered if Stephen was doing it deliberately.

"I didn't know you'd been here before," she said.

"When I was an undergraduate," he said briefly. "I sailed here for a few times from Cornwall. It's come in useful. I've been out with a fishing boat twice this week."

"It must have taken you at least a month to get this far," Stephen said. "How did you manage? What have you been living on?"

"What the hell do you think? A little housebreaking here

and there, a little light thieving from food shops. I even stole enough money one time to buy a train ticket, not all the way. I never rode as far as any frontier. I had to walk those. And if you want to know where I got these clothes"—he pulled at the sweater, backing away from them—"I made a few francs out fishing. One of the crew broke his arm. They actually paid me to replace him on the second trip. When they found out I was useful. And now I'm going to use them. That is, if you've thought of bringing any money."

He stood, yards away from them now, challenging them, angry, on the attack. *This is how he's stayed alive,* Julie thought. *He's lived on anger. This is what Stephen was probing for.*

Stephen said calmly, "Have you made any plans?"

"You're damn right I have. If I could have collected enough money, I wouldn't have needed you. But I can't wait. Every day is dangerous. I can't pay the bill for my room, for a start. I haven't eaten a decent meal for two days. I'm on the run, starving, and penniless, and you want a travel dossier on my happy holiday. Well, you got here, and I'm grateful for that, but if you'll just give me some money, you can take Julie back home, and I'll see you in England."

Stephen's air of cold detachment faded. He grinned. "Yes, I've got money. Lots of it. I smuggled some in. First time I've broken the currency regulations. Do you think MI5 will speak up for me?"

There was a silence in which Julie could hear a church bell in the town begin to chime, and then Richard's shoulders relaxed, his face changed, and he began to laugh, full, triumphant laughter like a man who has won a battle, and she rushed to him and hugged him, and he swung her around in a victorious dance while Stephen watched, smiling, and the seagulls, oblivious, walked the seaweed shore beside them on brittle spikes of legs.

They had a drink to celebrate. What? Their acceptance of him? The success of his campaign to reach friends, to draw them to his side? Richard kept his dark glasses on, and the barman made a joke about the brightness of the light in his shadowy bar whose windows opened on to the wall. Richard spoke equally lightly of a weakness in his eyes, and the barman nodded and said, yes, he knew of his illness. He was the convalescent, was he not, who was staying with Madam up the street?

"You see," Richard said quietly, "I've already been here

too long. I'm getting known. One question would find me now."

"How soon do you want to move?" Stephen asked.

"Tomorrow. I've been planning it, waiting for you. My part of it's all set, apart from the timing and the question of money. We'll arrange your passage today. There was a steamer would have done, but you've missed that. I think I can get someone to take you across for a fiver or so."

Julie was completely mystified. "Take us where?"

"One of the Channel Islands," Stephen said. "That's your plan, isn't it?"

"Yes. Jersey. If I can get ashore unnoticed there, my lack of passport, identity card, and so on won't matter. I don't need them to go to England from there. I can walk on the first boat."

"I see," Julie said. "That's very clever, Richard."

He shrugged. "If it's clever, it's because it's simple. There's only one risk, getting into Jersey. I don't intend to go at night, and chance running into a watchful coast guard. I want to land in daylight, in the afternoon."

"Your fisherman friends will drop you?" Stephen said.

Richard nodded. "They'll come inshore, putter along the coast. Now, near a beach I'll describe to you, I shall slip over the side and swim ashore. I want you two to be waiting, with a towel and a picnic basket, anything you like. To the casual spectator, we'll be a party, three hardy holiday-makers. You'll have to buy me some clothes—jeans and a sweater, sandals, a cheap raincoat, perhaps."

"You mean you're going to arrive like Venus from the foam," Julie said. "Clad in nothing but your dark glasses?"

He sounded almost shocked. "Certainly not. If you'll be good enough to cough up some of the illegal money you brought, I shall go and buy myself some bathing trunks."

She smiled. "I'm sorry, Richard. I know it's not a joking matter."

"I'll come up to wherever you are," he went on, "towel myself dry, get dressed, then we pack up, go to some hotel or boardinghouse for the night, and catch the morning steamer for Weymouth. They go every day now, about eight o'clock. You'll get the tickets before you meet me."

"Cut and dried," Stephen said.

"I hope so."

Stephen looked at Julie. "Is he a good swimmer?"

"I haven't the faintest idea. Are you, Richard?"

"Olympic class."

"In that case," Stephen said, "It'll probably work. I'm not very good. I wouldn't want to have to come out and rescue you from being swept away by tidal currents."

"On the beach I have in mind, it's perfectly safe bathing."

"All right then," Stephen said. "We'll try it. All right, Julie?"

There was nothing to do but agree. In the face of this efficient but somehow faintly absurd scheme, Julie was becoming sharply aware of the gap between herself and Stephen and her brother, the gulf that yawned between the deadly seriousness of the professional and the amused tolerance of the onlooker. And yet it was a deadly serious situation, and Richard's life was at stake. Perhaps it was the reaction of relief that was making them both behave rather frivolously. They could neither of them, even Stephen, have been absolutely sure of the result of their journey. They had not been certain, until they saw him on the ramparts, of the existence of this second Richard. And now they knew they had to face the implications of his existence, and one of the implications was that from now on it was going to be far more dangerous than ever before. This must be what was affecting her. She was obviously, Julie thought sadly, one of those who reacted to danger with a nervous giggle.

"I hope the weather holds up," she heard herself remarking. "We're going to look highly conspicuous picnicking in the rain."

Stephen looked at his watch. "Nearly one. I think we'd better eat something. Afterward we'll get a boat fixed for Julie and me, and I'll garage the car. I'll have to let them know in Dieppe where to pick it up."

"Don't ring from here," Richard said quickly.

"I'll ring from England."

Richard took off his glasses and rubbed his eyes again. "For the first time since I got away, I can really believe I am going to get back to England."

There was a pause. Stephen said, "We must tell you. There are complications."

He was immediately still. "What sort of complications?"

"They sent a man instead of you, two weeks ago. They exchanged 'Richard Davidge' for a man we were holding. He's been accepted by the security people, as far as we know. He's established in your flat."

Richard was silent for a few moments; then he said, "Now

that makes me really angry." He turned to Julie. "Does he look like me?"

"Yes. As you might have looked——" She hesitated.

He pursued it. "As I might have looked if what?"

"It's difficult to explain. I was going to say, if you had suffered that particular experience. What I really mean is that it's a brilliant performance. He's a very good actor. But he's too old. I can see that now." She glanced at Stephen. "I think I may have given myself away. He may suspect that I wasn't entirely convinced. I would have been but for your postcards."

Richard grimaced. "If they're taking such a risk with him, he'll have to be good. So that's the situation. I've not only to get back. I've got to prove I'm myself when I get there."

"Once you're back, they'll know you," Julie said. "Surely?"

"One man certainly will. I'm surprised he's been taken in. He not only knows me as a friend, he knows exactly what I've been doing and where I've been for the past five years. Once he gets around to interrogating him, I can't see the cuckoo staying very long in the nest."

With a faint sinking, Julie remembered Holbrook's words. She said, "One of the men who knew you very well, who worked with you, died last year. I don't know his name. But they thought it would upset you. They thought it explained a lot of things about the man who said he was you."

"Welford. Was the name Welford?"

"I don't know. I'm sorry, Richard, I wasn't told the name."

He put his head in his hands. "Damn," he said. "Damn, damn." He looked up. "What did he die of?"

She shook her head helplessly. She couldn't remember. She looked to Stephen. He had withdrawn once more into his detachment, leaning back, watching them without expression. She felt chilled. She wanted his warmth, his confidence that everything would be all right.

"They must have details of you, in files or something, that apply only to you. Physical descriptions, fingerprints, medical and dental records, and so on."

"If they've gone to the elaborate lengths of impersonating me, they'll have certainly dealt with all the relevant records. You'll find if you look in them everything which once described me had vanished. The records, fingerprints and all, will be his."

"Could they do that?"

"They'll have done it."

"You mean they'll have got someone inside?"

"I think it's more than likely there was someone inside already. The risks these people take are always strictly calculated."

Then you are in danger, she thought, *terrible danger. And so are we.* For the first time it really came home to her. She sat with her hands clasped together on the table in front of her, visualizing the web so intricately woven by deception and treachery. The people responsible were going to be careful to protect that web. From every eventuality. When Stephen had evaded that car in Caen, he had probably saved their own lives as well as Richard's.

She felt Stephen's hand on her wrist. "I don't think we should talk anymore here," he said quietly, and repeated, "Let's go eat."

Quite often during the next hour, Julie had the sensation of being a child again in the charge of adults. Richard, leading them to a restaurant where he said he had wanted to eat all week, began behaving to her like the kindly elder brother indulging the small sister in a treat, in a near parody of his own usual attitude toward her. He pressed her to try the shellfish and assured her, as if she might be diffident about her own greed, that he was going to eat his way through five courses. Since he hadn't eaten properly for days, she thought it likely that the drinks, on top of the tension of his situation, had gone to his head.

After a plateful of *moules marinière* and a couple of glasses of wine, the slight falsity of his manner eased. He began asking Julie about her own life, and she had the uncanny experience of repeating to him what she had already told his double.

"Michael who?" Richard asked, spooning more dressing over his tomato salad.

She had been telling him about her progress as an illustrator. "Michael Brent. You remember him."

"Yes, of course. I'm glad he's been of some help to you."

"I nearly sent him to see you—I mean, the other man. When Stephen and I realized there was a doubt. I thought he might have some personal recollections of you the man might not have been told."

Richard paused, fork in air. "Try to catch him out, you mean."

"Yes."

He glanced at Stephen. "Dangerous."

"That's what I thought," Stephen agreed.

"Did he go?"

"No, I decided not to ask him."

"But he knows what's going on?"

"I think he guesses something odd is happening."

"Does he know where my impersonator is living?"

"Yes."

"Do you think he'll go there to see him, anyway?"

It had never occurred to her. "I don't think so."

"But he might." ·

"Yes, he might."

He sliced neatly through his steak. "We'll have to stop him. I'll see him as soon as I get back."

"He might help you," Stephen pointed out, "with the identification."

"The way things are going, I'm going to need everyone from my nursery school teacher to the Archbishop of Canterbury to stand up and swear for me."

"Once you're back," she said, "once they've seen you—I mean, they don't even know about you. When they do, there won't be any question about accepting you. We've only got to get you back."

"That doesn't necessarily follow, Julie. There's bound to be some bright bastard, in fact I can think of several with no difficulty, who'll think we're pulling a fast one, trying to undermine the integrity of the sitting tenant by producing a pretender to the throne. If you'll excuse the mixed metaphors."

"They'll say you're the false one, you mean?"

He nodded. "And they'll be aided and abetted to the height of his influence by whoever is already inside. Not to mention the encouragement they'll get from the man himself. It's like a confidence trick. The ones who've been taken for the most are usually the ones who won't admit it. Nobody likes to admit being fooled."

"But they'll believe me!" Julie insisted.

Richard gazed at her for a moment. "Yes," he said at last, "you're right. You're my trump card, Julie. At least I'll get to see someone on the strength of a document from you swearing to the truth of my story. That, and seeing and talking to me, should be all they need. A sister knows her own brother, after all."

The implications of that hesitation of Richard's were not lost on her.

"Yes," she said ruefully. "You would think so."

He put his hand over hers. "Don't misunderstand me, Julie. I can understand how it happened. They are professionals, and they've deceived professionals. None of this is your fault."

But she was left with a feeling of stupidity and guilt.

Chapter 6

~~~~~~

When they had finished the meal, Richard said he would
go and arrange their passage to Jersey. He said it would be
better if he went alone. It would be quicker and less conspicuous. Stephen got the car out, and he and Julie drove out of
the walled town and went to find a garage where they could
leave it for collection.

He found a place finally at the far end of the sea front.
Juile waited outside while he completed the formalities. Out
here it was like any English seaside town: the long row of
small hotels and lodging houses, the bay windows giving the
promised view of the sea, the broad pavement on the seaward
side, the rounded metal railing, the steps cut down to the
shore, the cars and buses along the asphalt road to be dodged
by children swinging their spades. A green car went past,
but there were thousands of green cars in France, and anyway this one carried a family, with children and a dog.

She crossed the road and leaned on the railings. The windows of the houses looked blank and dead. Out of season.
An out of season resort, with a chill in the wind, and clouds

blowing up from the distant line of the horizon and the colors muted now and the sea the texture of oil.

Stephen came up behind her and put an arm around her shoulders.

"Don't feel guilty," he said. "You're not responsible for what's happened to him. He didn't consult you before he got involved."

She turned against him, and put a hand up and touched his cheek, cold from the wind. "I wish you weren't involved."

"Why?"

"I'm afraid for you."

"For me? I'm indestructible."

She looked past him at the road.

"I saw a green car pass just now."

"There are thousands of green cars in France."

"That's what I told myself. Anyway, it was full of children."

He kissed her.

"It will be all right," he said. "I guarantee it."

"I'm afraid for me, too," she said.

They were to meet Richard in a bar near the cathedral.

"He seems to know every bar in the town," Julie remarked.

"That's his training," Stephen said. "The first thing agents do in a new territory is walk every street and locate every bar." He smiled. "For suitable rendezvous. So I'm told." She could never tell when he was joking.

It was a small place, a long counter, a few tables and a juke box. It was empty. They ordered coffee and sat down at one of the tables.

"Do you think he'll find it difficult to get us a boat?" Julie asked.

"He seems to have established plenty of contacts. I don't think there'll be any difficulty."

"His training again, I suppose?"

"His training." He asked, "Do you find him much altered?"

She played with the spoon on her saucer, concentrating on it.

"Yes and no," she said at last. "The beard alters him."

"I meant his manner."

"I've never seen him under stress. But the fact that we've got here to help seems to be bringing back his confidence. He was always so"—she hesitated, searching for the word—"so definite. Assured and confident and adventurous. But not reckless. No, it's his self-assurance I remember most strongly."

"Remember?"

"I mean from my childhood."

"Did he always treat you in this way?"

"Which way?"

He frowned. "With that slightly patronizing air."

Julie smiled. "You know families. The gap between older and younger is never closed, for the older at least."

"No, I don't know families," he said. "I've no experience of them."

"There's another side to it," she said. "A protectiveness. They like to look after you."

"Did he look after you?"

"Yes. When he had time." She paused. "Do you find him altered?"

"I only saw him twice. My memory of what he looked like was very vague. I wouldn't have known him without you."

And yet, she thought, *he had said at once, seeing Richard on the ramparts, "There he is."*

The door opened. They looked up. A short, middle-aged man came in. He said good-day to them. He ordered a brandy and took it over to a table near the juke box. He put a coin in. A young French voice began to sing mournfully of the tragedy of life. The man sat down and began to read the paper, paying no attention to the music.

Julie said, "Did you really smuggle in money?"

"No. I had enough. With left-over business expenses. We're allowed so much a day."

"What about your job? Won't they wonder what's happened to you?"

"I've taken a week's leave."

She said, "It's generous of you to give up your holiday and put yourself in danger. Why are you doing it, Stephen?"

"First, I was intrigued. Second, I met you. Third, I like France."

"I wish you hadn't made meeting me a reason."

"Why not?"

"It makes me responsible for what happens to you."

He laughed. "You're the most extraordinarily responsible girl I've ever met."

The door opened again. This time it was Richard. He seemed displeased that they were not alone. He pulled a chair around so that he sat with his back to the man by the jukebox.

"Is it fixed?" Julie said.

"Yes."

"A fishing boat?"

"A motor cruiser."

"How long is the crossing to Jersey?" she asked.

"About three hours. It depends."

"I hope those seasick pills work in small boats."

"You'll be going at night."

She was surprised. "Why night? Why do we want to arrive in the middle of the night?"

"By night I mean four, five in the morning."

"Is it something to do with tides?"

"We've got a lot to do tomorrow," Stephen said. "We'll start off with a large breakfast as soon as we arrive. Then we've got to buy the steamer tickets, buy Richard some clothes, buy"—he smiled—"our picnic basket. Book somewhere to stay the night. Find the beach, find out how to get there, wait for Richard, no doubt running up and down to keep warm . . . "

She felt better. "I've a feeling we're more essential to the plan than he pretends. It's not just our money he's after, it's our footslogging capabilities."

"Speaking of money," Richard said. "They want some now before they finally agree. They wanted it all, but I said they could have half now and the rest when you get to Jersey. All right?" He stood up.

They both got up.

"Not you, Julie. You stay here. We shan't be long."

She didn't like that. "Can't I come?" She felt six years old again, deprived of a treat.

"No, only Stephen. He can make the final arrangements with them. We don't want all of us wandering around the harbor together, attracting attention." He repeated, as if he had suddenly realized she was nervous, "We shan't be long."

Stephen smiled at her. He followed Richard out.

If there was one thing Julie did not like, it was waiting for people for an indefinite time in bars. She bravely got up and bought herself another coffee. Since she took the cup with her, her French was understood. As she went back to her table, she saw that the man near the jukebox had lowered his paper and was watching her. She sat down where Richard had sat, with her back to him.

The music faded. The record had ended. A voice spoke in her ear. "You permit, mademoiselle?"

She jumped and turned her head.

The man was standing near her. He had a round, lined, rather sad face. His hair, what was left of it, was graying. Three or four strands had been carefully trained sideways to disguise the baldness. He was holding a coin in his hand.

He said in slow English, "The music does not disturb you?"

"No," she said. "Not at all."

He smiled and nodded with a certain eagerness. His teeth were not good. He had one gold one, which showed when he smiled. His gray pinstriped suit was tight. It looked as if they had grown old together. His shirt was clean and his tie defiantly gay. If she could have liked him at all, it would have been for his tie.

He went to the jukebox. He turned and called, "You have a choice, mademoiselle?"

She shook her head. He put the coin in. The bar exploded with sound.

He came back. He stood smiling down at her. "For you," he said. "English rock and roll." He pulled a chair out and sat down at her table. She realized he was choosing to take her first acknowledgment of his presence as an invitation. Unless she was deliberately rude, she was stuck with him.

"You are here on holiday?" he asked.

She nodded.

"With your friend?"

She decided an aura of legal masculine protection would do no harm. "With my husband."

"Ah—" It was a long-drawn-out breath that managed to include surprise, regret, congratulation.

"And the other," he said. "The fisherman. He is on holiday, too?"

She avoided a reply by sipping her coffee. She wondered if he called Richard a fisherman because of his beard and clothes or because he had seen him before. She wondered how much of their conversation he had overheard. She was becoming uneasy. She didn't like the man sitting there, nodding at her, asking her questions. His gold-toothed smile was taking on a sinister quality.

"Do you know the other man, our friend?" She attacked in her turn. He fell back in his chair, as if the question had literally flung him back with amazement.

"But no! Why should you think so? I only arrived in St.-Malo today."

"What are you doing here, monsieur?"

"My name is Brochet." He seized on the opportunity of introducing himself. "Paul Brochet. I am a salesman. I travel around the country."

"What do you sell?"

"Souvenirs. You know what I mean, madame. Ash trays, rings, cups, that sort of thing." He waved his hand to encompass the bar and the town beyond. "Souvenirs of St.-Malo, for example. Are you staying in St.-Malo long?"

She took a breath. "I thought they made souvenirs locally."

"Why, yes, occasionally, but even then there is the matter of distribution." He began explaining to her in great detail the complexities of his job. His car was parked nearby. His samples case was in it, if she wished to see the samples. She said it would be too much trouble. It was the wrong response. It would not be in the least trouble, he assured her. He was, on the contrary, anxious to show her. She said she had no time. Perhaps another time, he pursued. How long was she staying?

The question which she had ignored before was slipped in so quickly and casually it nearly caught her.

"About a week," she said.

He suddenly laughed. "I meant now, here, in this bar. Perhaps there would be time. If I fetched my case now?"

"I'm sorry," she said with unconcealed relief. "I shall be leaving now." She had seen Stephen and Richard at the door.

M. Brochet leaped up. He seized her hand and planted a kiss on it. "You are very beautiful," he said. "Forgive me if I have given offense. I envy your husband."

He slipped past the two men and out the door.

"What was that all about?" Richard said.

"He was a commercial traveler, trying to pick me up."

"Good Lord, he didn't waste much time." He was amused.

"No." She paused. "He asked me a lot of questions."

"Oh?" He sat down. "What sort of questions?"

"Who Stephen was, who you were, if we were on holiday, how long we were staying."

"That sounds like a normal opening gambit," Stephen remarked. He was standing with his back to them, looking across the square through the glass panels of the door. She wondered if he was watching Brochet.

"In any other circumstances, yes," Richard agreed. "You could call it normal curiosity. But these aren't normal circumstances. What else did he say, Julie?"

"Nothing very much. He told me about his job. He's a traveler in souvenirs. He said he'd only arrived in St.-Malo today. He's got a car parked near here somewhere. He wanted to fetch the case of samples to show me, so I suppose he must be genuine." She glanced at Stephen's back. She wished he would turn around. "Can you see him?" she asked.

He didn't reply. Richard said, "What impression did you get of him? Do you think he was genuine?"

She shook her head. "I don't know, Richard. I'm in such a state I'm suspicious of everybody. He could be perfectly genuine, perfectly harmless." She thought of the careful arrangement of hair, the bright tie like a flag against the faded suit. "I don't think he's very successful. He looked sad."

"He's harmless," Stephen said abruptly. He turned and looked at them. "There's no need to worry about him. When Julie is left alone, you must expect strange men to try to strike up conversations with her. If I'd seen her sitting alone, I'd have done the same." He came forward and picked up Julie's handbag and handed it to her. "Let's get out of here. You look as if you've had enough of it."

She nodded. Richard said nothing. She thought he remained unconvinced of Brochet's harmlessness. And so, in fact, did she. But then who was she to judge anyone's character by his face?

It was now nearly five o'clock. Richard remembered he had to buy bathing trunks.

"And a towel," Julie said. "I only brought a small hand towel."

They decided that while they were about it, they might as well buy the clothes he was to change into when he landed on the beach in Jersey.

Stephen stepped back. "You two go ahead. I'm going to have a look around the town. I'll see you at the hotel, Julie."

She watched him walk off across the square. She was aware of a sharp disappointment. It was irrational. Why shouldn't he go and walk around the town if he wished? No doubt he had a reason. He was hardly abandoning them.

Richard put a hand under her arm. "Tactfully leaving us for a family reunion, do you think?"

"Yes," she said. "Possibly."

"Very sensitive of him."

It was an echo of the words the other Richard, the false one, had used about Holbrook; about the man he suspected of watching him. The thought crossed her mind, to be dismissed as soon as formulated (for why otherwise would he have written to him?), that Richard did not like Stephen.

"Fortunately," Richard was saying, "I remembered to get some money from him. Let's get on with the shopping, shall we?"

As if the fact of choosing the clothes he would wear when he stepped ashore in England brought the prospect within the bounds of possibility, Richard's spirits rose with every minute. Julie could sense the growing excitement in him. It was a mood which was hardly affected even by the discovery that since it was Monday, most of the shops they tried were closed, as is customary in France. That put him off not at all. An obstacle as slight as that, she supposed, after all he had overcome was nothing to him. Seeing the owner working on his accounts at the back of one shop, Richard attracted his attention by tapping on the window and then coaxed and charmed him into opening up for what would be, he assured him, no longer than five minutes. They bought jeans, plimsolls, sweater, pants, swimming trunks in delirious haste, Richard calling to Julie to time him, beating the palm of his hand on his forehead in the effort to remember what he needed, and left with many flourishes of goodwill and the name of another shop where they might buy a towel.

Richard took Julie's arm in triumph as they came out, swinging the parcel in his free hand, rushing her up the sloping street between the wire-meshed windows and the pulled-down blinds and the calm provincial silence of the afternoon. He had been taken with the shopkeeper, an elderly and courteous gentleman with a stoop and a curving, piratical mustache. "Did you notice how his mustache curled up its ends at the sight of you? I must take you whenever I go shopping. You open doors."

He pulled her arm, and she stumbled and lost her shoe and went back for it. He stood at the top of the street, calling to her. "Come on, Julie, don't lag behind."

A cyclist spun around the corner, freewheeling down the hill. He turned his head to stare at them.

"For someone who believes in making himself inconspicuous—" She laughed.

"I'm supposed to have bad eyes. He'll think I'm waiting for you to see me across the road."

He never removed his dark glasses. "It leaves me with one more disguise in hand," he said facetiously. "I've only got to shave off the beard and whip off my glasses, and lo and behold, I've disappeared."

She said seriously: "You're quite happy about the plan? You can trust the fishermen?"

"As far as I know." He shrugged. "As far as I can trust anyone."

The linen shop when they found it was firmly closed, and this time there was no one inside to be lured into opening it again. As they turned the corner away from it, they walked, literally, into M. Brochet. He was carrying a suitcase, Julie presumed, though it seemed an odd time, with the shops shut, to be hawking samples. He backed away, apologizing. They walked past him. Julie resisted the impulse to look back.

"Your friend again," Richard observed.

"Not my friend."

"Not anybody's friend, I think."

It was impossible not to wonder if he had been following them.

They wandered around for a little longer, but it was obvious there was nothing more they could do about the other things they had meant to buy. Richard kept the swimming trunks and retied the parcel for Julie to take back to her hotel. They agreed to meet in the same restaurant where they had lunched, about nine.

"You should get some sleep," Richard said. "Try and rest till then."

They were both more subdued. They had not discussed it, but since the encounter with Brochet, the verve had gone out of the expedition.

Julie was crossing a street near the hotel when, through an archway, she caught sight of Stephen. She was about to call him when she noticed he was talking to someone. She walked closer until she could see right through the archway. It led into a courtyard surrounded by red brick blocks of modern flats. There were several cars parked there and standing beside one of them in animated conversation with Stephen was M. Brochet.

She saw Stephen smile. They shook hands. Brochet disappeared, and she realized he was getting into a car. She moved back. After a moment the car, with Brochet at the wheel, emerged from the archway and drove away up the street. Julie waited, expecting Stephen to appear through the arch. When he did not, she walked into the courtyard herself. He was not there. There was another exit on the opposite side that he must have taken instead.

She went back to the hotel room. She methodically packed her bag, putting the parcel containing Richard's clothes at the top. She washed her face and combed her hair. She didn't think about what she had seen.

Stephen came in about half an hour later. She told him what they had bought. She said they were to meet Richard at nine. He nodded. He sat on the edge of the bed watching her. He didn't say much. He was quiet, but it was not the quiet of tiredness or relaxation.

She began making up her face. "I saw you talking to Brochet," she said. "How did you come to run into him?"

"I saw him in the street," he said. "I followed him. I wanted to find out what sort of a man he was."

She looked at him in the mirror. "If he was genuine, you mean?"

"Yes."

"And is he?"

"Yes. We can forget about him. As you said, Julie, a not very successful salesman."

"What did he say to you?"

"He congratulated me on my beautiful wife."

"Is that when you smiled?"

"You're very observant. If you were so close, why didn't you join us?"

"I would have, but he drove away before I could, and then you—vanished."

He made no reply to this. She turned from the mirror. "Stephen, doesn't it seem strange to you that he should come here to sell his souvenirs on a day when the shops close?"

"I thought he was supposed to have just arrived. He's probably doing his selling tomorrow."

"Did you notice his car?"

"No, not particularly. Why?"

"It was a gray car. Do you remember the car that followed us out of Rouen? That was gray, with a man driving it."

"Julie—" he sighed. "Stop it. Stop that imagination of yours."

"But, Stephen, don't you see, there could have been two cars following us, one taking over from the other. The gray car and then the green car and then, perhaps, the gray car again."

He swore under his breath. He got up and came across to her. He took her hands and pulled her to her feet. He held her at arm's length, looking at her.

"Sometimes you look so guileless," he said, "I don't know how to cope with you. And I get frightened. I get terrified out of my life."

"But why? What are you terrified of?"

"Not of. For. I'm afraid for you. That you might be hurt. That I couldn't prevent it."

She tried to smile. "Now you're frightening me. What do you mean?"

"I don't know what I mean." He let her go. "I wish we were back in England. I wish you were safe."

"But I'm not in danger." She didn't want to hear the echoes of her own fears. "No more than you. Stephen, it's Brochet, isn't it? You do believe he's something to do with them—"

"Julie, stop it!" His voice was sharp. "Forget Brochet. Forget him. Don't talk about him." He picked up his coat. "I'm going out. I'll be back before nine." He paused with the door half open. He looked back at her. "I didn't mean to frighten you. Try to rest." He closed the door behind him.

They had both told her to rest. Both of them. She lay on the wide expanse of the bed, smoking a cigarette.

A fly, awakened to sluggish life by the treacherous April sun that morning, was crawling over the white wastes of the plaster ceiling toward the magnet of the lighted bulb in the center of the room. The globe that shaded the bulb had not lately been cleaned. Two or three dead flies were visible through its base, the fallen black bodies of earlier explorers.

Julie watched the fly. After a while, she swung her stockinged feet onto the carpet, walked to the door, and switched off the light. The blue-gray dusk invaded the room. The fly was lost in the shadows. It no longer mattered if it moved or not. She felt better. As if there might now be one victim less.

She poured some brandy into a glass and sipped it. Still holding the glass, she leaned on the windowsill, gazing toward the sea and watching the night drain the color from the sky. It grew quite dark. She lay down on the bed again. Now the only light in the room was the pale rectangle of the window. She could hear the sea, breaking and withdrawing and breaking, a lulling, soothing sound. She closed her eyes.

She awoke with a start to a flood of brilliant light. She struggled dizzily up on one elbow. Stephen was at the door, his hand on the switch.

"You looked very sweet," he said. "I'm sorry to wake you."

The light hurt her eyes. She lay back on the bed with her arm covering them. She was aware of him coming toward her. He sat on the bed and leaned toward her; he rested on his arms, his hands placed flat on either side of her body.

He said casually, "You didn't lock the door."

She moved her arm and looked up at him. "You didn't tell me to."

He smiled. "And do you do exactly as I say?"

She studied him gravely. "I trust you," she said.

The dark gray eyes watched her, seriously, reflectively. He bent his head and kissed her throat.

"You should trust nobody," he said. "Not even me."

They dined at the same restaurant and sat at the same table as they had at lunch. The quality of the food was as good, but none of them had any appetite.

"I overburdened my stomach with my greed this morning," Richard remarked. He pushed his plate away and poured himself more wine. Stephen took the bottle from him and refilled Julie's glass.

"Are you all right?" Richard asked her. "You look pale."

"It's the thought of the sea crossing," she said. "That's all."

He lifted the dark glasses with one hand and rubbed the bridge of his nose. The glasses seemed to be troubling him.

"Take them off," Julie suggested. "It's safe enough here."

"Ah, but you never know when M. Brochet might pop up with his box of souvenirs."

Julie looked down at her plate. "Stephen talked to him," she said. "He thinks he's what he says he is."

"That's interesting," Richard said. "Why?"

Stephen was not to be drawn. "He's innocuous," he said briefly.

Richard nodded. "If you say so."

Stephen got up and went to pay the bill. The proprietress, a woman in her forties, all rounded figure and professional charm, evidently found him attractive. She engaged him in conversation, her ringed hands holding the notes of his change in the air, out of his reach. Julie heard her asking if they were yachtsmen, as she put it, who had sailed over from England.

"You see," she remarked to Richard. "Everyone asks questions. It's natural."

Richard took her glass of wine and poured it into his own. "You didn't want this?" She shook her head.

He sipped the wine, watching Stephen. "How involved are you with Stephen Archer?"

The question took Julie by surprise. "Very involved."

"I thought you must be." He put the glass down. "I didn't intend to play Cupid when I sent those cards. How much do you know about him?"

"Not very much."

"Neither do I."

The proprietress laughed, a consciously musical ripple of sound. She put a restraining hand on Stephen's sleeve.

Julie said, "Why did you choose Stephen if you knew so little about him?"

Richard shrugged. "I was desperate. I had to find someone to help you. I didn't want you going to the police or the security people. I knew if you let them know, the others would know, too. I went to Lyons to send the card because I thought it would confirm that it was from me. When I was there, I remembered Archer. His name and address flashed into my mind, the way these things do. It was a calculated risk. And yet, now I'm beginning to think about him, odd things come to mind. Small things. Just that he was in Lyons and started an acquaintance with me and that it was in Lyons I was kidnapped. The night we had dinner together for the second time."

Julie stared at him. "You don't think——"

He ran his finger around the rim of the wine glass. "I don't think anything. He did nothing, after all. Except perhaps"—he raised his finger and put it down gently on the glass—"put the finger on me."

"You mean, point you out to someone?"

"Identify me. Yes."

"It's ridiculous," she said. "Impossible. Think of all he's done to help."

"Naturally. He would have to, if he wanted to find me."

They had both instinctively lowered their voices. *Whispering like conspirators,* she thought with distaste. She glanced at Stephen. He stood with his head inclined politely toward the woman, listening to her. She knew him well enough, Julie thought, to recognize the impatience behind the controlled pose.

"You've forgotten the car," she said. "The one that followed us to Caen and that he got away from."

"Perhaps the getting away was deliberate, to put you at ease."

She felt a wave of indignant denial. "Richard, I don't believe it. I know it's not true."

He nodded. "I agree. I think it most unlikely that it is true. But, Julie"—he put his hand lightly on her wrist—"you must learn not to be so trusting. Because someone is attractive to you, it doesn't mean he is trustworthy. If you expect people to betray you, you won't be caught out when they do."

"You talk exactly like an elder brother," Julie said.

"Do I?" It seemed to amuse him. He grinned. "I'll try not to."

He stood up as Stephen finally extricated himself and came back toward the table. "But nevertheless," he murmured quietly, "this business of Brochet is puzzling, isn't it?"

It was about ten thirty when they left the restaurant. Stephen had paid the bill at the hotel. Their bags had been left downstairs, ready for them to collect any time before one, when the proprietor locked the place up for the night. It had been arranged that they could go on board any time after twelve. The boat would be waiting for them from that time on. They had two hours or so to waste. They began walking a little aimlessly in the direction of the Grande Rue.

It was dark, damp, but no longer cold. At least, Julie, warmed with food and wine and apprehension, no longer felt cold. The wind had dropped, or perhaps it was that the walls protected them, that the wind did not penetrate beyond that barrier.

At night the walled city had a medieval air. Julie had the sense of a community withdrawing, with the onset of darkness, behind its defenses; looking now inward, not out to the sea and the world beyond, but to itself, to its own particular interests and pleasures, its own feuds, which it would practice within the limits set and regulated by itself and defend with a fierce inherited group loyalty.

Perhaps it was an illusion. Perhaps she only felt it because it fitted her sense of entrapment, the theatrical drama of the lurking unknown danger that might strike at any time from the shadows. And that night the city was a place of shadows, of silences, footsteps, laughter heard from a distance, voices, silence again, and the footsteps that were their own as they walked together without speaking.

Julie walked between them, one arm linked with Richard, one with Stephen. They were alike in their concern for her. They had warned her not to trust, both of them, as they had earlier told her to rest. She found it difficult. She had not made a choice. She had acted from instinct from the beginning. She had had to. The whole affair had been an exercise in blind faith. She did not know how to stop.

She unlinked her arm from Stephen's and sought for his hand. He gripped her hand, the fingers interlocking with hers, with a grip that hurt at first, before he relaxed it. They did not look at each other.

The laughter had grown louder. There was another noise too, a murmuring of voices, and the unlikely sound of music at night. By common consent they turned, curiously, toward it. They crossed a street and saw a crowd approaching and heard the throbbing of a drum. They stood with their backs to the shop windows and heard the unmistakable shout of a trumpet. A band passed them, the polished instruments gleaming under the streetlights; a brass band with its instruments held upward to the sky, blaring in triumph, the feet stamping and hats on the back of heads, sweaty faces blown and red, here and there a collar undone of the braided, polished-button uniforms they wore, uniforms of no color in this light but none more braided and polished than that of the man who walked in front carrying a rod like a mace of office which he held high and waved occasionally from side to side in stately, dignified sweeps. The crowd wandering happily around the band obscured at first the cart that followed it, a cart bedecked with branches and ribbons and carrying a straw-lined wooden cage in which stood, with a garland around its neck, a small white pig.

Richard suddenly laughed. "Fertility rites?"

"Let's follow," Julie said. "Let's see where they're going."

They went everywhere and nowhere. They wound about the city streets, cart rolling along behind, in a curling, trailing, noisy, haphazard procession, the same tune endlessly repeating itself, soaring and thumping and growing ragged, the tempo speeding and fading and gathering pace, the drummer thudding monotonously, carried away, all carried away with an enthusiasm that overcame failing wind and drying mouths and sagging, tiring arms, and still Julie could not find out what they were supposed to be doing.

Stephen and Richard asked their neighbors in the crowd.

"It's a celebration!" they were told.

"And the pig?"

"Oh, the pig!" And then smiles and shrugs and jokes. No one, it appeared, knew why the pig was there.

At last, as if their strength could take them no farther, the band came to a halt in an open space beside the wall. They shook their instruments and wiped their faces and coughed, and arranged themselves in an orderly manner beside the decorated cart and began to play their tune once more.

"They're serenading the pig," Julie said.

"After which they'll eat it," Stephen remarked.

A woman standing next to them laughed and said something which Julie missed. Richard began talking to her in rapid French. He turned back to them grinning.

"She says you're quite right. They probably will eat the pig. It's the prize. They've won a local band contest, and that's the spoils of victory."

"Oh, no, poor pig!"

At that moment the streetlamp behind the band went out. People near it looked up and moved away, colliding with each other. The band was making too much noise to hear what they were saying, but something was obviously going on. People were looking up at the wall. A group of young men broke away and went leaping up the steps to the ramparts.

"What is it?" Julie said.

The band stopped playing. The musicians looked around, puzzled, asking questions. There was broken glass on the pavement. The lamp had been shattered.

"It was shot out," Richard said. He glanced at Stephen, frowning. Stephen was engaged in conversation with an elderly man who was expressing his views with a good many emphatic gestures.

"He says it was done by boys with an air gun," Stephen reported back to them. "On behalf of the losing team. He saw them running along the wall. He considers it the French equivalent of not playing the game. He says they won't have any trouble catching them. I hope he's right. It's a bloody silly thing to do, showering glass over everybody."

Richard had taken hold of Julie's wrist. He was looking beyond her, behind them. Suddenly he jerked her back, away from the light, against the wall of a house.

"What is it? What's the matter?"

"We're getting out of here. Stephen, we're getting out!" He pulled Julie through the crowd, past the bewildered band, around the corner into a darker street. He didn't look to see if Stephen was following. Halfway up the street was a lighted bar. He pushed Julie inside. After a moment, to her relief, Stephen joined them.

"I suppose there's a reason for this," he said mildly.

"Yes." It was an abrupt reply. Richard went over to the bar counter. Stephen looked at Julie. "We might as well sit down."

Richard brought back three glasses of cognac, bunched together precariously in his hands. The proprietor, who had risen reluctantly from a group of men to serve him, went back to his friends. In a thickening pall of cigarette smoke, amid a litter of empty glasses and full ashtrays, they were playing a desultory game of cards. They looked around at the newcomers and, uninterested, went back to their game.

Richard clattered the glasses down on the table and sat down. "I asked him when he was closing. He said when everyone's gone, so we can stay here for a while."

Julie said, "What time is it?"

"About eleven thirty."

"Do you mean to say we've been following that damned pig around for nearly an hour?" Stephen smiled at Julie. "No wonder I'm exhausted."

"Why did you make us leave?" she asked Richard. "Because of the air gun?"

"The first shot was from an air gun," he said. "The second wasn't."

She stared. "The second?"

"I didn't hear a second shot," Stephen said.

"That's probably why he risked it. No one could hear anything with that noise, not unless it went whining right past your ear."

"Richard!"

"It chipped a bit out of the wall. If we went back, we could probably find the bullet."

"He?" Stephen asked.

"I looked in the direction from which it had come and

who should I see among the crowd of merrymakers but our peddler of souvenirs."

"Brochet?"

Richard nodded. He drank down half his brandy in a gulp.

"Coincidence," Stephen said. "I should think everyone in the town came out to see what was going on. No one could miss that band."

"I don't care if it's coincidence or not," Richard said. "I don't care who fired the shot. The point is someone did, and that means they know I'm here."

"Yes, you're quite right," Stephen said. "The sooner we get you out the better."

"We ought to split up. Two men and a girl are easier to find than one man. I'm used to making myself invisible. Take Julie to the boat right away."

"I don't think we should leave you," Julie said.

"No, he's right," Stephen said. "He's safer on his own."

"What will you do?" she said. She couldn't bear leaving him alone again, in worse danger.

"Stay here till they close up, then get down to the fishing boat."

"What if they look for you in here?"

"They won't." He grinned. "But if they do, I'll hide behind them." He nodded at the card players. "Another half hour and you won't be able to see across the room for smoke." He put his hand over hers. "Don't worry, little sister. I'll be swimming ashore tomorrow as large as life."

She squeezed his hand. "All right. Look after yourself."

She didn't want the brandy. She pushed it across to him. They left him sitting at the table. She looked back as they went out of the bar. He wasn't visible from the door. That reassured her a little.

They went back to the hotel and picked up their cases. No one appeared to follow them or show any interest in them. They left the old town by the Porte de Dinan. Julie stayed in the shadow of the wall while Stephen walked along to where it had been arranged the boat taking them to Jersey would wait. He came back to her. "They're there, I'm glad to say, and it's all right to go on board. You might as well get some sleep. We won't be sailing for a while."

It was a smaller boat than she'd visualized. She realized that the distance was at least as far as from Dover to Calais, and she wouldn't have fancied crossing the Channel in this craft. She said nothing. She went aboard and shook hands with the owner. To make things less cramped she went obediently into the cabin. Stephen stayed above.

"I want to keep an eye on things," he said. "You never know."

After a while one of the crew brought her a mug of coffee liberally laced with brandy. She drank it, hoping the brandy in it might knock her out or at least stop her from thinking. It didn't work. She was wide awake and stayed wide awake. It was a relief when at last the engines were started up and they nosed their way out of the harbor into the open sea.

It was a terrible crossing. There was a pitching, falling motion which continued with sickening regularity. The engines smelled; the cabin was stuffy. She lay on the bunk and tried to practice a little self-hypnosis. The pills against seasickness had been lost somewhere. She felt it was not the thing to do to make a fuss. Stephen came down to see her once, and she managed to talk normally to him. By sheer force of will she refused to be sick.

They came into St. Helier at half past six on a cold clear morning. Julie had forgotten they would have to be inspected by customs and immigration. She let herself be guided along by Stephen. He put his arm around her. "All right?" She nodded. She was beyond speech.

The customs official was a jovial man in a talkative mood. "You're bright and early," he said. "First customers today. Excitement get too much for you?"

"What excitement?" Stephen said.

"I was just hearing about it. They fished a body out of the harbor over there. Haven't had that happen for a good long time."

Richard, Julie thought. She gripped Stephen's arm.

"What happened?" he asked. He sounded casually interested.

"It was in the small boat harbor. Two Dutch boys going back to their yacht after having a meal in the town saw something in the water. Hauled him out. Quite dead. They think he was a visitor, belonged to one of the boats moored there perhaps, had too much wine, not used to it, tripped off the boardwalk, and bingo! Probably knocked himself out as he fell. No one about. Some celebration going on in the town, they said. Everyone was watching it. They let us know. Might be a day tripper from here, you never know."

"We didn't see anything," Stephen said.

"Probably all over before you left. Staying long?"

"No," he said. "Not long."

They got away in the end. By nine they had booked rooms in a hotel, had washed, changed, and were having breakfast. Stephen insisted on Julie eating a proper meal.

"It is Richard, isn't it?" she said. "They shot him."

"They didn't shoot him, whatever they did. The customs officer would have mentioned that. And I don't believe it was Richard."

"But he'd have to go down to the harbor sometime. They'd know that. They must have been waiting for him."

"Listen, Julie. We got to the boat about twelve. There was no sign of anything then, no police, no crowd. And nothing happened from then until the time we sailed. So it must have been before twelve. The customs officer said the man was found by two boys going after a meal. Even if they ate late, they'd probably have been back by about eleven. There was a celebration going on at the time, he said, remember? We were there watching it, weren't we, all three of us? When Richard saw Brochet and took us off to that bar, it was eleven thirty. Richard couldn't have run down to the harbor after we left, got knocked on the head, drowned, and then been found, hoisted out, and carried away all in the fifteen minutes or so it took us to get to the motor cruiser. So it's proved. Richard is alive and well and no doubt knocking back the brandy with his fisherman chums this very moment. Now eat up your eggs,"

"Stephen, we were quite a way from the yacht harbor. You wouldn't necesarily know what was going on there."

"I was on deck for most of the time before we sailed. I think we'd have heard something, lights, shouts, ambulance, if the body had been found after we got there. It was a coincidence, that's all. Very unfortunate and sad for the poor man who drowned but nothing to do with us. You look terrible, you know. Try some good old English tea."

She smiled.

"That's better," he said. "You can collapse when we get back to England, but not now. I'm feeling worn-out myself. I shall need your shoulder to lean on."

After breakfast they walked through the town and bought a towel for Richard to dry himself with when he came ashore. They also bought a cheap holdall to put it in. They had coffee in a tea shop and read all the English papers.

"I feel as if I've been away for weeks."

"Two days," Stephen said. "I wonder what's been happening to the other one, the other Richard Davidge."

"They know now, don't they?" Julie said. "Will they be waiting for us?"

He didn't answer. He folded the paper. "Come on, let's go and buy a map."

The bay where Richard intended to land was difficult to get to, off the beaten track, the bus route, and everything else. "I can see why he chose it," Stephen said, "but it doesn't make things any easier for his fellow conspirators, does it? We'll just have to hire another car."

He emerged from the hire office smiling, the keys of a minicar in his hand. "Everyone here is very amiable," he remarked. "They think every visitor they get in April must be on honeymoon. I told him we were desperate to get away from all those other couples, and he practically reduced the fee."

The roads they drove along in the early afternoon were pretty and deserted. The air had warmed, and the sun endeavored to shine.

"Would you like to come here for your honeymoon?" Stephen asked.

She glanced at him. He was smiling as he drove. He looked sideways at her.

"Are you asking out of general curiosity or to get specific information?" she said.

"If that's your devious way of asking if I'm proposing to you, the answer is yes. What's yours?"

"Yes."

"Good," he said. "That's settled."

They drove on in silence for a while.

"You really do believe Richard is still alive, don't you?" Julie said.

He took her hand. "Yes, darling, I do."

"I knew you weren't the sort of man to ask a girl to marry him if he thought her brother was dead."

"What's that got to do with it? I'd ask you to marry me if everyone was dead. I love you."

"That's the first time you've said that."

"Well." He paused. "I don't like to rush things."

She laughed. She bent across and kissed his cheek. He raised her hand and kissed it. Everything seemed wonderful, marvelous, possible. All dangers fled away.

After that, it seemed impossible for anything to go wrong. They parked the car near the beach and walked down to it and sat on the sands, smoking, and gazing at the horizon. They didn't look very much like a party of picnickers, but it didn't matter. There was not a soul in sight.

The fishing boat came, not over the horizon, as Julie had somehow expected but around the point of the next bay. It was quite far out. It looked perfectly normal and natural and as if it were going about its rightful business.

"That's a long way to swim," Julie said.

They got up and walked down to the sea. The fishing boat was halfway across the bay. She realized it had turned slightly and was heading farther out to sea. "He must have left—"

Stephen pointed. "There he is." He looked back along the beach. It remained empty.

It took Richard ten minutes to swim ashore. It was the longest ten minutes Julie had known. When he got near, she waved and shouted. He waved back. As the water grew shallower, he got to his feet and began wading in. She didn't care who was watching. She went splashing out to him. She flung her arms around him and hugged him. He was cold and wet as a fish.

"I think the damn tide's on the turn," he said.

They got back to the beach. Stephen threw the towel to him, and he wrapped himself in it. He was grinning and trembling at the same time. "God, I'm frozen. Never again. Next time, I'm coming over by submarine." He jerked his head back and closed his eyes and mouthed something silently as if he were saying a prayer. He opened his eyes and looked at them.

"I hope you two have got some brandy," he said.

At two forty-five the next day they landed at Weymouth. By eight o'clock they were in Julie's flat.

Chapter 7

~~~~~~

She awoke at ten. At first she couldn't think where she was or whether it was night or morning. The curtains were drawn. She got out of bed and went to the window and pulled them back. Daylight. A nondescript day, neither uplifting nor depressing, just gray light on a London street. She could hear from above the faint tapping of the agency typewriters. From the window she saw a man walking down the street toward the house. Stephen. She pulled on her dressing gown and went into the living room.

Richard had piled his sheets and blankets neatly at the end of the sofa. He had cleared away the ashtrays and the glasses she had been too tired to deal with last night. She found him sitting at the kitchen table drinking a cup of coffee.

"I think I've ruined your reputation," he said. "I came galloping out of the lavatory in my shirtsleeves and bumped into some old girl coming upstairs. I could positively feel her eyebrows soaring when I nipped in here."

"I expect that was Miss Dawson from the agency upstairs. She's rather sensitive about her lavatory."

"Like some coffee? It's hot."

"Lovely." She got two more cups and saucers from the cupboard. "Stephen will be here in a minute. I saw him from the window. Did you sleep well?"

"Like a felled oak."

"I thought the sofa would be too short."

"After some of the places I've slept, it felt like the great bed of Ware." He stretched his arms wide. "There is, to quote the poet, no place like home."

He no longer wore his dark glasses. He had taken them off as soon as they were safely in the flat. His eyes were bright. He looked rested and full of vitality.

"You look as if you've been on holiday," Julie said, "not moldering in medieval dungeons."

"That's what a little freedom does for you. Take a dose of freedom every day, ladies and gentlemen, and you'll be a new man. Marvelous for the circulation."

He raised his cup to her and said, "Thank you, Julie, for fetching me home."

"Don't be serious, Richard, or I shall start my sentimental weeping all over again." Though she hadn't cried when they found him, she remembered. It was the other Richard she had wept to see. Tears of shock and relief and pity.

That other Richard would know now. Or perhaps he didn't. Perhaps they had no way of reaching him with the news. The real Davidge had been seen in France. The real Davidge had escaped to England. The real Davidge had been shot. Was that the news he waited for, sitting in the flat in Regent's Park, drinking the gin Holbrook allowed him, eating his ham sandwich without mustard? It must be terrible to be cut off, to know if you had failed only by the faces of the men they sent to arrest you.

"What did we finally do with the letter?" she said.

"I've got it," Richard said. "I slept on it."

"And how does it read now you've slept on it? Is it all right?"

He added. "It should open the door."

They had spent most of the previous evening drafting the letter that was to be the first step in the establishment of Richard's identity. It was difficult to know what to put in and what to leave out; whether it should be a full account of everything that had happened since the arrival of Richard's first message to Julie or a brief and succinct statement that they'd got the wrong man and she'd got the right one.

Stephen suggested that Richard might also send a statement, but Richard decided against this. What he was after was the direct confrontation. When they got Julie's letter, they'd have to investigate her claim. They'd have to see the man she was producing as her brother. That was all he'd need.

They decided on the brief statement. When finished, it was arresting enough to arouse anyone's curiosity. It said without preamble that the man exchanged as Richard Davidge was not Julie's brother, that her brother had got in touch with her, that she had met him and identified him beyond all doubt. As one attempt had already been made on his life, she would be glad if action could be taken at once and a dangerous situation averted.

Julie wrote it out and signed it. The next thing was to decide whom to take it to. Richard was concerned about Welford's death. The inevitable changes in the department left him in a state of uncertainty. He was unsure who it would be best to approach. When he hesitated, Julie suggested she find out the telephone number Dorothy had been given and ring that. She thought that would bring her in touch with Holbrook. He knew her. She could talk to him. She would ask for an urgent appointment, without specifying why. Richard agreed. She was to ring Dorothy this morning.

It was, strangely enough, the first time Dorothy's name had been mentioned between them. Richard made no further comment on her. He asked no questions as to her health or situation. He seemed totally uninterested in his wife. Julie wondered how Dorothy was going to react to the news when she heard it. She had a suspicion that she would consider it merely another example of Richard's tiresomely selfish habit of getting involved in complicated and troublesome situations.

Richard didn't know Holbrook, at least not by name. "I might recognize him when I saw him."

"He knows you," Julie said, "by reputation anyway. He's got a high opinion of you."

"That's nice," Richard said. "Perhaps he'll be my friend at court."

The doorbell rang, and Julie went to let Stephen in. He had spent the night at a hotel. He hadn't discussed it; he had simply gone, leaving her and Richard to rest. She thought he could have done with more rest himself. He looked tired and tense.

She kissed him. "I saw you coming. Take your coat off and have some coffee. I've only just got up."

"How's Richard?"

"Full of euphoria."

"Is he? I should think he'd be worried. This is his most dangerous day, after all."

"That's a cheerful start to the morning."

"I mean I should think they'll try to stop him, wouldn't you, Julie? From getting to that 'direct confrontation' of his."

She paused. "Yes, I know. Now I think of it, it's surprising they didn't try something last night."

"Yes."

"Or do you think they hadn't realized he'd got to England?"

"Possibly."

"We're not very bright, are we? We should have posted sentries or something. We could have been murdered in our beds."

He looked at her without speaking.

"Is that why you're looking so worried?" she said.

"You're his identity," he said. "Don't forget that."

"Oh, God, now you've really wakened me. Don't frighten me any more."

"All right." He smiled. "Where's this coffee?"

While Stephen drank his coffee, Julie went to bathe.

"Have you rung Dorothy yet?" Stephen asked as she came out of the bathroom.

She shivered. "Not before I've got my face on. I need all my strength."

He glanced across at Richard. "Did Julie tell you your wife's reaction to your impersonator?"

Richard looked up. "No."

"She told Julie he was behaving in a most peculiar fashion. She told her he wasn't the same man as the one who had left England."

Richard laughed. "Good for Dorothy. Once married, never forgotten, that's me."

"It might help," Stephen said. "She'd probably identify you at once."

"I've no wish to see her again. Except as a last resort."

"Wives might be even better than sisters, as far as the security people are concerned."

"They might be, but she won't be necessary."

Stephen shrugged. "Did Mr. Morfitt see you when you came in?" Julie asked him.

"I don't think so. I didn't notice."

"The grocer downstairs thinks Stephen is a policeman," she explained to Richard. "We had a petty crook snooping around. Morfitt had let one of the cellars to him. Stephen went out and put the fear of God into him."

"What sort of a crook?" Richard asked.

"Oh—" She hesitated. "No one important. We decided it was all a false alarm. Well, I'd better get dressed."

She went into the bedroom and shut the door. She sat on the bed and lit a cigarette and smoked it, inhaling the smoke. She felt nervous, and she wasn't sure why. Because of the danger? The threat that was to herself as well as to Richard? No, something more, something more. Indefinable. Currents of unease. She went to the window and looked out. She did not know what she was expecting to see. Men with guns waiting for them, waiting for the attack? It was like being besieged. The threat was intangible, unseen, but constant. She thought of the shot fired at Richard in St.-Malo. Not so intangible.

There was nothing to be seen in the street. She made the bed and got dressed. She found Dorothy's number in her diary and went into the living room to telephone. Stephen was standing looking out of the window. She wanted to laugh. Their reactions were so alike. He turned around. She picked up a pen and a rough sheet of paper.

"I'm going to pounce on her," she said. "Not give her the chance to vacillate."

"Dorothy?" he said. She nodded. She dialed the number. Richard came in from the kitchen and leaned against the door. They waited.

The number rang for a long time. As Julie was beginning to accept that she was out, Dorothy answered.

"Dorothy, it's Julie," Julie said briskly. "David Holbrook asked me to ring him this morning, and I've mislaid the number. Could you give it to me, please?"

There was a pause. Dorothy said: "Do you mean that number? The one they gave me—"

"Yes, that number." Julie made her voice sound firm, unequivocal. She said nothing more. She waited.

"I'll have to get my bag," Dorothy said at last. "Hold on." She went away.

Julie put a hand over the mouthpiece. "She's getting it." Richard winked at her.

Dorothy came back to the phone. She read the number, and Julie wrote it down.

"What does he want to talk to you about?" Dorothy asked.

"I don't know. I shan't know till I've rung him."

"Have you seen Richard again?"

"No," Julie said. "Have you?"

"No. They seem to be keeping him as secret as the grave. I rang him up. I said I'd come to see him. I thought I should, after all. He said he was being allowed to see no one. Security reasons. It's all very mysterious."

How could the man have expected to survive in the long run? Julie thought. *With even Dorothy suspicious of him.*

"I'm surprised to hear from you," Dorothy was saying in her slightly barbed way. "I thought you'd be too concerned with that other business. I did ring you yesterday as a matter of fact, but you weren't in. You sound quite calm, I must say. I thought it might be quite an upset for you. Did you hear how it happened?"

"How what happened?" Julie said. "What other business do you mean?"

"Don't you know? But didn't you see it in the papers? It was on television, too."

"See what, Dorothy?" Her hand tightened on the receiver.

"It is the same man, isn't it? He had the same name."

Julie closed her eyes. She said patiently, "Who had the same name? Who are you talking about?"

"That friend of Richard's. That artist you said was helping you. Michael Brent. It was in the papers. He was in an accident at the office. The lift fell down the shaft. He's dead."

Afterward she realized she had been acting in a state of shock. For the first ten minutes or so she did not know what she was doing. Stephen told her she let the receiver drop, left it swinging from the end of its flex with Dorothy's voice calling plaintively from it, and walked out of the room. She was aware of the walls of the house as she walked down the stairs. They seemed very narrow. They pressed in on her. She was aware of the cold air on her face as she walked along the pavement. She found herself in a taxi with the driver looking back at her through the glass. He was telling her why they had arrived. She gave him a large tip, almost as large as the fare. She walked into the building. Her mind was blurred. Her heart beat in her throat. There was a heavy padlock on the gate of the lift. She walked up the two flights of stairs and into Michael's room. As soon as she entered the room, her mind cleared and she knew why she had come there. She remembered what had happened.

Anne Latham was sitting at her desk, staring at a pile of folders in front of her. She looked up at Julie. She did not seem surprised to see her.

"I'm tidying up," she said. "Sorting things out. They're trying to keep me busy."

"It's true then," Julie said.

"Yes."

Julie sat down. "I've been away. I've only just heard. When did it happen?"

"Tuesday. Tuesday night."

"Anne—Anne, what *happened?* I was told it was the lift."

"Yes. Mr. Lockwood's terribly upset. He's blaming himself. He says they should have scrapped it years ago. But the firm's only the tenant here. It's really the landlord's responsibility."

"Did the cable break?"

"I don't know. I don't think they know yet. They had engineers here all day yesterday. I heard they thought it might be some part that was worn, that happened to go at that moment." She broke off. She opened a drawer and took out a tissue and blew her nose. In the course of the morning she had wiped away all the makeup she had started out with.

"All I know is," she said, "I shall never set foot in that lift again, no matter what they do to it."

Julie looked at Michael's desk, at his chair, at the things on the top of the desk: a leather blotter, a jar of pens and pencils, erasers, cigarette box, ashtray, a calendar in a case that flicked over one day at a time. Anne had put clean blotting paper in the folder, she had sharpened all the pencils, she had arranged everything in a neat line. She had not altered the calendar. The date was that of Tuesday. Seeing the desk made Julie want to cry.

She said, "Mike never set foot in the lift. He never used the lift. He always used the stairs."

Anne said, "I told them that. When they told me what had happened, I said, 'Mr. Brent never used the lift.' They said, 'Well, he did this time.' "

"Then you weren't here when it happened?"

"No, I'd gone home. I always left before him, at five

thirty, to get my train. No one was here. He must have been working late. They think he was the last to leave."

"He didn't often work late, did he?"

"No." She shook her head. "No. He didn't need to. He seemed disorganized, but he wasn't really. He was always up to date with everything. He was very clever. He was so kind. He was so nice to work for—" She stopped.

Julie looked down at her handbag. She clasped it tightly with both hands. She heard Anne blowing her nose. She looked up. Stephen was standing in the doorway.

She let out a long sigh of a breath.

"Michael's dead," she said.

He came into the room. "I know. I got it out of your sister-in-law before I let her off the phone. I thought you must have come here."

"This is Stephen Archer," she said to Anne. "He's a friend. Anne Latham, Michael's secretary."

Anne nodded.

"I'm very sorry," Stephen said to her. "It must have been a terrible shock."

"That lift," Anne said. "Everyone complained about it. Everyone knew it was jumpy. But no one thought—" She broke off.

"I saw some men working on it when I came in."

"How did you know where to come?" Julie asked.

"I looked the firm up in the phone book. Then when I got here I wandered around until some kind girl found me and showed me the way."

"We're always finding people wandering around," Anne said. "There's never anyone downstairs in Enquiries. I think they spend all their time drinking coffee." She seemed calmer, as if the presence of other people was helping her.

"Would you like some coffee?" she asked. "I can easily make you some. They've got a kettle next door."

"Thank you," Stephen said. "I think that's a very good idea."

She got up, relieved to be able to perform a service for someone again. She was lost without a center to her life: at work, Michael, at home, her husband. It was her nature to look after people.

She paused at the door. "Did he manage to get in touch with you, Julie? He tried twice on Tuesday. He said he would try again in the evening." Her voice faltered. "I wonder . . . I mean he might have rung after I'd left. Before—"

"I don't know," Julie said. "I was away." She glanced quickly at Stephen. "Do you know what he wanted?"

Anne shook her head. "No. No. I think he said some family matter." She went out.

Julie stared across at Stephen. "Stephen—"

"Yes. I know what you're thinking: Did he go to Richard's flat?"

"A family matter. That could only mean Richard. It's my fault. I shouldn't have said anything. I made him curious. I even told him where the man was living. Stephen, he must have gone there. He must have found out. I had an instinct." She beat her fist down on the arm of the chair. "I had an instinct not to tell him!"

"Wait here," Stephen said. "I'm going to talk to the engineers."

She opened her handbag and took out her cigarettes. She lit one and smoked it, walking restlessly about the room. She did not know what to do with the ash. She looked at the ashtray, clean and sparkling on Michael's desk. She tapped the ash into the metal wastepaper basket.

On the far side of the desk she saw several illustrations resting against the wall, each protected by its veil of fine paper. She lifted one up and found it was her own, the last one she had brought in. He must have been looking at it on Tuesday. She shut her eyes tight. She felt such a pain of loss she did not know what to do.

Anne returned with a tray of coffee. She spoke Julie's name. She put the tray down and came over to her and gently took the illustration from her and put it down where it had been. She grasped Julie's hand and led her to a chair.

"Sit down," she said quietly. "Drink some coffee; you'll feel better."

Julie sat down and obediently sipped the coffee. She realized that she was angry. She was astonished that she was capable of such feeling. When Stephen came back she said almost eagerly, "Well?"

"They don't know," he said. "They say they can't tell. They were considerably shocked at the thought that anyone might have damaged the lift deliberately."

Anne sat up. "Surely you don't think—"

"What exactly do they think happened to the lift?"

"As far as they can tell, a part sheared off and that led by chain reaction, as it were, to the final collapse. They are rather puzzled that it should happen at all, that's plain. It's an old lift, and there has been trouble with the mechanism—"

"That's certainly true!" Anne said.

"But they say it has been regularly inspected, and a failing such as this should have been picked up before it got to that point. However, as one said to me, there is such a thing as human failing. It could have been overlooked."

"Someone helped it along," Julie said.

"It could be," he agreed. "I don't suppose we'd ever be able to prove it."

He opened the door and looked up and down the corridor. "No one in sight. Every door is shut." He patted the door. "Good solid wood. I should think these offices are quiet, aren't they?" Anne was staring at him with complete incomprehension.

"Yes," she said. "They need to be quiet, this sort of work."

"You could walk about this place all day without a soul bothering you. If they did scc you, thcy'd only prcsumc you were one more visitor who'd lost his way. I've just walked right to the top, where the lift mechanism is, and no one challenged me. The engineers thought I was a member of Lockwood's staff."

He looked at Anne. "Was there anybody wandering about on Tuesday? Did you see anyone you didn't know in the corridor, for instance?"

She shook her head. "No, I don't think so." She thought about it. "There was a man looked in Tuesday afternoon. Just put his head around the door, you know. He'd come to the wrong office. He was looking for the accounts department. I sent him upstairs to them."

"Ah—" Stephen leaned against the desk. "Was Michael Brent here at the time?"

"Yes. He was sitting at his desk."

"Which faces the door," Stephen observed.

"Yes, but what would that mean?" Julie said.

"I should think it means that the man who came to kill him had never seen Michael. He didn't know what he looked like. So he came to have a look at him. Make sure he got the right man. Did he ask whose office it was, by any chance?"

"Yes, he did," Anne said. "He said could I tell him whose office was this, and I said Mr. Brent's, the art editor, and he shook his head and smiled and said wrong again, and apologized for disturbing me. I asked him which department he wanted, and he said accounts, so I came to the door and told him how to get there. He thanked me and went off."

"What did Michael do when the man came in?"

"Nothing. He glanced up, I think, and then went on with what he was doing. The man spoke very softly."

"But you went out into the corridor with the man? You had a good look at him?"

"I suppose so. I didn't pay him very much attention."

"What was your impression of him? Who did you think he was?"

"I thought he was a clerk from some firm. Especially when he said he wanted accounts. Come about invoices or bills or something. I didn't think about it."

"He looked like a clerk?"

"Yes."

"Wearing an ordinary sort of suit, plain tie, that sort of thing?"

"Yes, I suppose so. I didn't really notice. He had a coat on, I think."

"Anything about his face? Could you describe him?"

Anne looked doubtful. "It was an ordinary sort of face. You wouldn't look at him twice."

"Thin or fat?"

"Oh, thin."

"Long nose, short nose?"

She shook her head. "I'm sorry."

"Dark or fair?"

"Middling, I suppose. Brown hair, you know. Ordinary. Brushed straight back from his forehead. Receding."

"How was it receding?" Julie said suddenly. She got up and took a notepad from Anne's desk and one of the newly sharpened pencils. She sketched quickly and held the paper up to Anne. "Was it receding at the sides, leaving a point, like this?"

"That's right," Anne said. "Like that."

"And did the rest of his face look something like this?" She drew in firm rapid strokes. She showed the drawing to Anne.

"Yes," Anne said. "That's just like him. Do you know him?"

Julie looked at Stephen. "It's Robinson, Morfitt's tenant, Mr. Robinson."

There was no doubt now in their minds that Michael had been murdered. It was relatively easy to reconstruct what must have happened. His curiosity aroused, Michael had gone to see Richard at the Regent's Park flat, probably on the Monday. He had simply walked in and rung the bell. It must have surprised the man in the flat very much. They had no idea how much he knew about Michael's friendship with Richard Davidge, but it was obviously not enough. Somewhere during that meeting Michael had caught him out, in a lie or a lack of knowledge about something he would have known if he had been the man who went to college with him and shared digs with him. He had also, fatally, given himself away. The man knew he had made a mistake. He knew Michael was not deceived. He must have had some way of contacting his friends outside because instructions had been given to stop Michael's mouth.

On Tuesday, Michael had tried to ring Julie. On Tuesday, Robinson had come to the office off the Strand. He had made a reconnaissance and discovered in the ancient and unreliable lift an excellent excuse for an accidental death. He found Michael's office and identified him. He fetched whatever he needed to put the lift out of action, came back to the building and waited. He waited until Anne left at five thirty. He waited until Michael finished for the night and came out of his office. Somewhere along the corridor, between the office and the stairs, he struck Michael down. He hid his body until he was certain the building was empty. The cleaning of the offices, Anne had told them, was done in the morning, not in the evening. Michael had been working late, so Robinson would not have had long to wait before it was safe to move. He put Michael's body in the lift and took it up to the top floor. He completed his work on the lift mechanism. He walked down to the basement and rang the bell for the lift. It began to descend. The movement sheared the weakened parts completely away, and it fell five stories to the basement. And that was that.

They did not tell Anne the whole story. It was not possible to do so. It would have put her in danger as well to know about the two Richard Davidges. They tried to reassure her. And it was not too difficult, for Julie could see that Anne did not really believe that the lift had been deliberately damaged. She could not accept that anyone should want to kill Michael.

Stephen asked her to say nothing, not even to her husband,

about the man who had lost his way to the accounts department. He said he would be speaking to the police, and it
would be unwise to discuss it before then. He said he must
take Julie home.

"Why don't you go home, too?" he suggested. "I'm sure
they won't object."

She shook her head. "They told me to stay at home for
the rest of the week if I wanted. But I wanted to come in.
I wanted to be busy. It's easier to be busy. It helps you get
over the shock."

Stephen and Julie went downstairs. They got a taxi at
the top of the street.

"I keep seeing him," Julie said. "Lying broken at the
bottom of that shaft."

"Don't think about it," Stephen said. "This isn't the time
to think about it."

"Do you think he was dead when he put him in the lift?"

"Yes, I'm sure he was. Julie, he wouldn't have known anything about it. A blow on the head!"

"That's worse," she said. "That's even worse. What right
has anyone to do that. To kill someone. Suddenly, treacher-
ously, without warning. Alive, then dead. Death shouldn't
be like that."

He put his arm around her. She buried her face against
his chest.

"I killed him," she said. "It's my fault. I killed him. I
killed him." She kept repeating it. Stephen stroked her
hair. She began to cry. He didn't try to stop her. He let her
cry. She was still full of this terrible anger.

As they approached the flat, she sat up and wiped her
eyes. She said, "Robinson's got a key to the house. Morfitt
said he wasn't taking his things till Saturday. We shouldn't
have left Richard."

"He'll be all right," Stephen said. "Richard can look after
himself."

"He was sent to keep watch on the flat, wasn't he? Robinson, I mean. In case Richard came there. I wonder why he
tried to get inside the flat?"

"To tap the phone probably. Wire the flat."

"Do you think he put anything at all in the cellar?"

"Morfitt said electrical equipment. I should think he was
right. He probably had some kind of radio down there to
communicate with."

"With the Regent's Park flat? Is that possible?"

"I don't see that it's impossible."

"So they've known as much as we have."

"They didn't know Richard was in St.-Malo. They wouldn't have needed to follow us if they had. Robinson had left by the time I came down to London with that last card, hadn't he? I wonder why."

"I think he got frightened off by the agency girls," Julie said. "He must have thought he was getting too conspicuous. He must have decided to do his watching from outside after that."

"It's contradictory," he said. "There's something wrong with it."

She passed a hand over her face. "I hate that man," she said wearily. "I could kill him myself."

They turned into Julie's street. Stephen asked the driver to go to the end of the street and turn left. They passed the house and drew up around the corner outside two telephone kiosks. Stephen got out. He put his hand out to Julie to help her down. She stood on the pavement, her legs feeling as weak as if she'd been ill, while he paid off the driver.

"Why have we got out here?" she asked him. "Aren't we going back to the flat?"

"Yes, in a moment. I want to make a telephone call. I remembered these phone boxes." He paused. "I rang you from one of them, the first time I spoke to you."

"Oh, yes . . . I remember. 'I'm five minutes away,' you said. 'Around the corner.'"

"I never tell a lie," he said. He smiled at her.

"The beginning of it all," she said.

"Julie, are you all right?"

"Yes, I'm all right. You go ahead." She looked at the kiosks. "It's surprising they're both unoccupied. They're probably out of order."

He opened the door of one of them. "You're right. This one is broken. God, what a stench." He let the door go quickly. "Some drunk's refuge."

The second telephone was in working order.

"You think Robinson is listening in to my phone?" Julie said.

"Let's put it that I don't feel the flat is all that secure at the moment."

She leaned against the side of the box while he made his call. It did not occur to her to ask who he was telephoning. She was still half dazed with shock. She kept seeing Michael.

Glimpses of him. At the PR party eyeing the statuesque blonde; in his office, encouraging her about her work; at his club the last time she had seen him sitting reading his paper, looking so strangely vulnerable. She could hear his voice in her head, laughing, making jokes. He was a kind man, Anne was right. That was the quality you remembered about him. He had liked her and been kind to her, and she had killed him.

Stephen pushed open the door of the kiosk and came out.

"Have you finished?" she said brightly.

He looked at her without speaking. He shook his head. "I don't know what I can do about you," he said. He looked at his watch. "I wish the pubs were open. You need something strong to shake that mask from your face."

"What mask?"

"Oh—" He shrugged. "You look like one of those beautiful carved effigies on medieval tombs. Cold marble."

She put a hand involuntarily to her cheek. "I'm quite warm."

"Oh, Julie—" He smiled. "I love you."

She tried to smile back. "That's the second time you've said that."

"Yes. It's becoming a habit."

He drew her hand away from her cheek. "You didn't kill him, Julie. None of us killed him. He was murdered. And we are going to catch the men responsible. I promise you that."

He met her gaze steadily. Steady gray eyes Richard had told her not to trust.

He had that calm, serious, observant expression she had first noticed about him. It was a characteristic expression. He was a man who made no concessions. She wondered how much detachment there was behind those eyes.

He linked his arm with hers. "We'd better get you back to the flat. And I want you to stay put till I return."

She stopped. "Aren't you coming back? Where are you going?"

"I'm going to see David Holbrook in half an hour." He took a piece of paper out of his pocket and gave it to her. "You'd better have this back. It's the number Dorothy gave you. It does reach Holbrook. I've just tried it."

"You mean you're going to take the letter? Tell Holbrook about Richard?"

"Yes."

"What will Richard say?"

"I don't know. We'll find out. He's got the letter."

Richard seemed disconcerted by the idea.

"Holbrook's never seen you. Do you think he'll believe you?"

"Why not? I shall have Julie's letter. That's all he needs to take action."

"But he won't know her handwriting. He won't know it's genuinely from her."

"I shall tell him enough to get things moving, don't worry," Stephen said. "I'm not letting Julie go wandering around London with a letter like that in her pocket. It's far too dangerous. Surely you agree? After what happened to Michael Brent?"

Richard glanced at Julie and back to Stephen. "I suppose you're right. But do you think this flat is any safer than the street, after what you've found out?"

"I don't think anywhere is particularly safe at the moment, but the flat is as good a place as any. The house is full of people. I don't think they'd make a move until it was empty. But they might try something in the street if you went out."

"What did you say to him?" Julie said. "On the phone. Holbrook, I mean."

"Enough," Stephen said. He seemed to be being deliberately vague. "Enough to get him to see me."

"He was suspicious of the man already, I'm sure," Julie said to Richard. "So he would listen."

"All right," Richard said. "Someone's got to go." He handed Stephen the letter. "Let's hope we're doing the right thing."

"Don't use the phone," Stephen said. "I mean to try to speak to Holbrook. I don't want to be intercepted on the way."

"I think I can grasp the dangers of using the phone," Richard said dryly.

Richard did not speak for a while after Stephen left. He sat with his hands clenched between his knees, head bent, frowning in thought. Julie moved quietly about the flat, tidying things up, avoiding disturbing him.

At last he came to her, where she stood in the kitchen cleaning out the sink. She had washed and put away the coffee cups. The sink was not particularly dirty, but it was something to do.

"I wonder if we've made a fatal mistake," Richard said. She turned to look at him.

"He's got the letter," he said, "and we're here, in a flat with only one exit, in a house with one staircase and one door to the street. In a trap."

"Robinson's got a key to the front door," she said.

"Get rid of us, destroy the letter, and they're safe."

She put the dishcloth and cleanser down carefully and rinsed and dried her hands. "What do you think we should do, Richard?"

He shrugged. "Wait. They won't do anything till the house is empty. He was right about that. Why should they? They don't want to attract attention. And they know we'll stay put. He told us to."

"Richard, I don't believe that Stephen—"

"Don't you? Don't you really, Julie? You came back just now and told me what you'd found out at Michael's office. The man Robinson and the lift. You said you thought he'd learned about Michael's visit to the Regent's Park flat from the man in residence there, that he'd established communications with him from the cellar here. Do you really believe that? Do you think the security boys aren't watching and listening to everything that man in the flat is doing? They'd do it anyway for his protection, for a week or so at least, as a simple routine matter. The other side must know they'd pick up something like odd telephone calls to a bookmaker, or a dentist, or whatever kind of code they'd agreed on, and check it till it fell to pieces. Can't you see it's simpler than that? Stephen Archer was with you when you talked to Michael. He could see he was curious. Perhaps Archer didn't do anything then; I believe he didn't do anything till I put it into his head in St.-Malo, but then he acted fast. Do you remember me asking you if Michael might go to the flat because he'd realized something odd was going on. Well, I saw Archer's face then. I think he rang Robinson from St.-Malo."

"Richard—"

"Well, what other explanation is there? And now this insistence on taking the letter." He slapped his hand down on the table. "He never rang Holbrook at all! He probably rang Robinson or whoever else they've got over here working with them. He'll have torn the letter up as soon as he got out of the door. He'll have gone to some hideout and be waiting for news, the news he'll expect to get tonight, that the threat to their man is over."

He saw her face. "He won't be coming back, Julie."

She sat down at the table and put her hands over her face. "I don't believe it."

He came to her and gently pulled her hands away, making her look up at him.

"I know you love him," he said, "or you think you love him, but that's what they do. They use emotion when it'll work for them. He made love to you because it suited him, it bound you to him, made you determined to believe him. Don't be a fool, Julie."

She stared up at him. She said nothing. He let go of her hands and turned away.

"I'm sorry," he said. "I'm very sorry you are involved."

"I'm not dead yet," she said. "Like Michael."

He swung around. "Yes," he said. "I'm sorry about Michael. It's the nice people who get hurt in this game, Julie. The nice, innocent people."

"Well . . ." She pushed the hair back off her forehead. "What do you want us to do about all this, Richard?"

"Have you got some girlfriend you could stay with for a night?"

"Yes, I suppose so. If I rang—"

"You can't ring. We can't use this phone."

"I know two girls who share a flat in Kensington. They'd put me up in an emergency. There's no guarantee they'll be in."

"You can ring them from a tube station when you're on your way. Give me the number before you go. What time does the typing agency upstairs finish?"

"Five thirty."

"Right. I want you to leave when they do. Talk to them, walk to the bus or the tube with them. All right? Go to your friends and then wait till you hear from me. Don't try to get in touch with anybody."

"What are you going to do?"

"I'll leave twenty minutes after you."

"Won't they be waiting for you?"

"I don't think so. They think we trust Archer. They'll have someone watching the flat, but they won't be prepared to do anything. They'll have to make decisions. I'll get away, don't worry."

"And then what?" she said.

"I'll go to Regent's Park. You told me the security chaps had taken over the flat below."

"Yes."

"Right. I shall knock on the door and introduce myself. They'll have to hold me for investigation. We ring you, send someone to fetch you back to identify me, and there we are. It's probably what we should have done in the first place."

Julie got up. She went back to the sink and turned on the taps, swilling the water around to remove the last traces of the cleanser. She wrung out the cloth and hung it up. She dried her hands and put the towel back. When she had finished, she had made up her mind.

"I'm sorry, Richard," she said, "I don't believe it. I don't believe Stephen is an enemy. I think he's taking the letter to Holbrook. I think he's coming back, long before nightfall. He told us to stay put, and I'm going to do what he says. I think you are wrong."

Richard sat down. He clasped his hands together in an almost desperate plea. "He spent a lot of time in St.-Malo on his own. What was he doing, Julie, do you know? We know that he talked to that commercial traveler, what's-his-name——"

"Brochet," Julie said. "He was called Brochet."

He nodded. "That's right. Stephen was very anxious to protect him, wasn't he, from our unfair suspicions? He was genuine, he told us, quite innocent. And yet it was Brochet who tried to shoot me. Doesn't that shake your blind faith, just a little bit?"

"Richard . . . " It was almost a cry. "You've got to trust somebody. I trust him."

He raised his shoulders in a gesture of frustration and irritation. "Julie, you're an idiot. Don't you think I know more about these things than you?" He studied her face. "Well, do this for me at least." He sighed, as if his tolerance was fast evaporating. "Take the precaution of going to your friends in Kensington. Get out of this house. It's not safe here. I'm telling you this, elder brother to younger sister. Now do this for me. Do something sensible for once. Will you?"

"All right," she said. "I can see the sense in that. I'll take myself out of the way."

He relaxed. "Well, that's something. Good. Thank you." The thanks was ironic.

The doorbell rang.

It was amazing how circumstances could give sinister connotations to the simplest of things. After the alarms and horrors of the day, the sound of her familiar bell aroused a moment of plain panic in Julie. She had to pull herself physically together to overcome it.

"Don't answer it," Richard said.

"It might be—"

He shook his head. "It can't be Stephen Archer. Even if you were right about him, it would be too soon."

It rang again.

"I can't stand it," she said. "I'm going to see who it is."

"Julie—"

"There's a chain on the door," she said. "I'll put the chain on."

He followed her into the hall. She slid the chain into its socket and edged the door open. Richard retreated into the shadows. Julie peered around the door. She met the slightly surprised glance of Margery Dawson.

Julie smiled. "Just a moment." She closed and unchained the door and opened it again. "Miss Dawson, I am sorry. I was being careful."

"I don't blame you, my dear. Though I believe that Mr. Robinson has gone now, you know. I haven't seen him about."

"Good, good."

"I got your note. Did you have a good time away?"

"Yes, thank you."

"You weren't gone very long, were you?"

"No." It was almost antisocial not to relieve a little of her curiosity. "It was a working trip. To do research for an illustration."

"Oh, I see. Research." She accepted that with respect. "I hope you were successful. Nobody appreciates the amount of work that goes into these things, do they?" She produced a bundle from under her arm. "Here are your newspapers. I brought them down. I don't think there was any post for you." She paused. "I thought you must be back when I saw your friend this morning."

"Yes. I've had a relative staying overnight."

"Oh. A relative. Oh, I see. Well—" She smiled with the brightness of a girl guide determined to think the best of everyone. "See you soon, then."

"Yes, and thank you very much."

"Not at all, dear, not at all."

Julie closed the door. She gave a whoop of laughter. "Did you hear that, Richard?"

He had gone back into the kitchen. "Yes. Who is that old girl?"

"She runs the agency upstairs. She kept my newspapers for me." She dropped them on the table. Miss Dawson's normality had broken the sense of tension. She pulled a newspaper toward her. "How ancient day-old newspapers seem."

"Do you know what time it is?" Richard said.

"No, I've lost count of time. My watch has stopped."

"It's five past four, and I've had nothing to eat all day. Would there be anything in the cupboard?"

She folded the paper and pushed it to one side. She had come across the report of Michael's death.

"Bacon and eggs, something like that? Simple?"

She looked up. "Richard, I'm sorry. Of course, I'll make something. I didn't think. I'm not hungry."

"No?" His expression was concerned. "But perhaps you should have something before you leave."

"Yes," she repeated. "I'll make something."

He nodded. He casually picked up the paper she had been looking at and went into the living room. She heard him striking a match for a cigarette.

Julie gathered up the rest of the papers and put them on a stool out of the way. She wiped the surface of the table, then opened the fridge and got out eggs, bacon, and butter. There were tomatoes in a bowl on the bottom shelf. She took a couple out, held them a moment in her hands, and then put them back again and closed the fridge door. She put the kettle on for tea and took the heavy frying pan down from the shelf by the cooker. She stopped, with the pan in her hand. She put it down on top of the stove and went back to the fridge. She opened it and looked at the tomatoes. She felt a cold terror move in her stomach. She felt the fear and the knowledge spread through her body like a paralyzing drug. A moment ago she had picked up those tomatoes and then unthinkingly, automatically, replaced them. She knew now why she had replaced them. It was because she wasn't hungry, because she wasn't cooking the meal for herself. She thought of Richard in St.-Malo eating lunch on the day they had found him. Eating his *moules marinière* and his steak and his tomatoes. Her brother couldn't eat tomatoes. He had never been able to eat tomatoes. He was allergic to them. They made him ill.

She put her hand to her mouth. She made herself breathe slowly. She went to the door of the living room. She didn't dare go in in case he looked up and saw it in her face. She swallowed and said as easily as she could: "Would you like some tomatoes with your eggs?"

"Fine," he said. "Anything you like."

She got back into the kitchen and closed the door behind her. She sat down at the table. It was all confusion and fear and a paralyzing inability to think. Think! She must think. It didn't fit. None of it fitted. What about the postcards? What about the car that followed them to St.-Malo, the attempt on his life by Brochet, Michael's murder? She must be wrong. He must have got over his allergy.

Love apples, he'd said once, were wrongly named for him because to eat them poisoned him.

She had known him when she saw him in the flat, the day Holbrook took her there. Her first instinct had been right. His laugh, the way he threw back his head, his way of talking. The compassion she'd felt for him in his suit that was too big, with his bony face and suffering eyes and stubbornness.

The man in the next room had never been imprisoned. "You look as if you've been on holiday," she'd said. And there was the way he had run carelessly through the town when they went to buy his clothes. He didn't care who saw him. He knew no one was after him.

And yet, Brochet had shot at him. And yet, he had been so nervous he never removed his glasses. Or was it that he was too careful, in spite of his exhilaration at their acceptance of him, to risk removing that concealing mask of glass?

"Next time," he had cried on the beach in Jersey, "I'll come by submarine." And had shut his eyes and sworn at himself for the stupidity of that evocative phrase.

Felled ox, she thought. *The phrase is felled ox, not felled oak.* And who called anyone a chap, these days? Security chaps. And why had he never once called Richard's flat "my flat"? It was always "the Regent's Park flat." Such small things, a gradual accumulation of small things which she had unconsciously noticed and filed away and which had begun to make her uneasy; but not until they were back, safely in the flat and he had taken off those glasses because to keep them on any longer might cause suspicion. They were not Richard's eyes. No, she was sure of that now. They were not her brother's eyes.

"What's the matter, Julie?"

She had not heard him come in. He spoke from behind her.

"Julie, are you all right?" He came around and stood in front of her. He was holding the newspaper in his hand.

She said, "There was something in the paper, about Michael. It upset me."

He nodded, as if she had solved a puzzle for him. "So that was it. I wondered."

She realized he had taken the paper and searched through it for some small item that might have given him away. What could possibly be in the newspaper about him? Even if the news about Richard, the real Richard's exchange had leaked out, that shouldn't alarm him.

"Don't worry," he was saying. "I can do it myself."

He was talking about the meal.

"Why don't you lie down for half an hour?" he suggested. "You look very white."

She said she would. She got up, and as she passed the stool, she picked up the other papers. He glanced at them but said nothing. She went into the bedroom and spread the papers out on the bed and began going through them.

She found it in the morning's paper. It was on an inside page, just a filler, three lines of an agency report. It stated that the man found drowned in St.-Malo harbor had been identified by the French police as M. Paul Brochet, a sales representative.

There was no more. It was not a story of much interest to English readers.

Chapter 8

~~~~~~

Julie sat on the edge of the bed with the newspaper in her hands and read the item again. The man drowned in the harbor had been fished out and taken away long before she and Stephen had got there at midnight, a good half hour, at least. The customs official in Jersey had made that clear.

If she had wanted confirmation of her suspicions, there it was. Brochet was already dead when Richard claimed Brochet had shot at him in the St.-Malo street.

She still called the man Richard in her mind because she had to identify him somehow, but it was a Richard with a different flavor now, a Richard III of a name associated with cold-blooded murder for political ends, colored with death and darkness.

He must have seized the opportunity of the air-gun attack by those boys to stage a little drama of his own. It had been important to him to confirm that he was in danger, to convince them that Brochet was something more than an innocent salesman. Why?

It was quite clear now—because of Stephen. He thought Stephen suspected him, and he, in his turn, suspected Stephen of being, if not an agent himself, then working in close association with Holbrook and his friends.

Stephen must always have been their weak point. There was always the possibility that he would take Julie and the carefully planted postcards straight to British security. The false Richard had worried about that so much he had convinced himself it was true. There had been Stephen's aggressive interrogation when they met. And when that was successfully over, there was the appearance of the salesman asking questions, and Stephen's defense of him. Brochet, Richard must have thought, was working for the British; and so he had killed him.

Julie was just as sure he had murdered poor Brochet as she was that it was on his instructions that Michael had been killed. The story he had given her was true in one respect. It was a phone call from St.-Malo that had resulted in Michael's death, but it was Richard who had telephoned Robinson, not Stephen.

How much, she wondered, did Stephen suspect? He must have had some doubts in St.-Malo, but perhaps they weren't strong enough for certainty. He hadn't recognized Richard, but after all, she, his sister, accepted him. He had been afraid that Brochet, whom he took the trouble to assure himself was no more than he seemed, might be dragged into the circle of suspicion because of the questions he asked. "Leave Brochet alone," he had warned her. Had she, with her wild imaginings, been responsible for that death, too?

But Stephen didn't yet know that the body in the harbor was Brochet, so perhaps he now believed in this Richard. Perhaps the shooting incident had wiped out his suspicions. In that case, he would be taking that letter of identification to Holbrook, and she would be left as the one person who knew the truth. If anything happened to her, that letter would remain as her voice; and it would be a doubly convincing statement if the writer were dead. It had become the most important factor in the whole affair. "Remember you're his identity," Stephen had said.

What was going to happen to her when she left the house at five thirty? Who was going to follow her? What accident would be staged for her? Could they possibly dare to leave her alive after the identification had been established? Who knew what small mistakes he might make in the future, what slips he might have already made? It was too big a prize to let a risk like Richard's sister remain alive. Suppose they brought the two Richards together, suppose she was able to talk to them both, at length. Wouldn't there be something the real one knew that had been omitted by ignorance from the briefing of the wrong one? Like an allergy to tomatoes. They hadn't dared risk it with Michael. They had killed him without knowing anything about his interview with her brother, just on the off-chance he might ring her and tell her there was no doubt in his mind about the man exchanged, and so start her wondering and questioning.

She had to tell someone. She had to get to a phone. Then she had to come back here and stay put. She mustn't leave at five thirty. If they hadn't come to rescue her by then, she'd have to pretend she was ill, anything, but she mustn't be out on those dangerous streets alone. The man in the next room didn't know she suspected him, she had that much advantage, but it was clearly of the utmost importance to him to get her out of the house before Stephen and Holbrook arrived. Stephen's insistence on going must have brought back all Richard's fears of him. The plan must have been speeded up. It was to have been her word plus the letter, with the accidental death coming later. Now it was going to be the letter alone. Her mouth was to be shut before any detailed questions could be asked. That was behind his attempts to get her to doubt Stephen, to make her afraid of him, to get her to leave the house.

She had never imagined that she could think about her own death so dispassionately. *I'm still in a state of shock,* she thought. She got up from the bed and looked at herself in the dressing-table mirror. She looked ill. Her face was white and her eyes feverish. She took a piece of cotton wool and her makeup cleanser and wiped off what little makeup she had on. She took an eyeliner and drew a dark line along her lids. She brushed some lilac eyeshadow, which had never suited her, on her eyelids. She combed her hair severely back from her face and tied it in a ribbon. In the glass, huge shadowed eyes stared from the pale face. Any doctor would have handed the owner of that face a medical certificate at the mere sight of it.

Her handbag was on the chair. She took out the paper with the vital telephone number on it, her door keys, and enough change to feed the telephone. She put it all in a handkerchief held loosely in her hand. She opened the bedroom door.

He was standing outside, holding a cup of tea.

"I thought this might help," he said.

She swallowed. "Thank you, you are kind. I'll have it in a minute. I'm just going below. I'm not feeling very well. The crossing upset me. You know what a bad sailor I am."

There was an instant's nerve-racking pause. She felt him studying her. But why should he doubt her? She carried no handbag. She looked awful. She did suffer from seasickness, and one of her friends had been murdered. There were plenty of reasons for her to be feeling ill.

He nodded. "I'll take the tea back to the kitchen."

She closed the bedroom door behind her and went out of the flat. She walked slowly down the stairs. When she reached the lavatory on the landing, she opened and closed the door with what she hoped was a loud enough click for any listener to be satisfied. She waited on the landing. There was no sound from above. She counted to ten under her breath and then crept downstairs. Through the glass door of the grocers she could see Mr. Morfitt cutting ham for a customer and chatting garrulously away. She got safely out of the house.

Once in the street she kept close to the houses so that she could not be seen by anyone glancing out of the window. She walked to the end of the road. About halfway up, a man came out of a doorway opposite and crossed the street in front of her. He was walking quickly with his head down. He disappeared around the corner. When she turned into the street where the telephone boxes were, the man was just closing the door of the one that worked.

He seemed for a moment not to know what he had gone in there for. He looked at her through the glass. Then he turned away and dialed a number. He put a sixpence in and started speaking. He looked out at her as he spoke. She turned her back. When she looked again, he had put the phone down. She moved forward with relief. She felt very exposed standing out in the street. She waited for him to come out. He was rummaging through his pockets. He produced a small black notebook that looked like an address book, opened it out, and laid it on top of the shelf that housed the directories. Beside it he piled a small supply of sixpences and shillings. He picked up the receiver and dialed another number.

She couldn't bear it. She knocked on the glass, trying to attract his attention. He ignored her. He was tapping his sixpence up and down with his free hand while he waited for his number to come through. She hoped it was engaged or unobtainable, but even if it was, she could tell he would simply go on to the next number of an enormous list. He was going to be there all night.

Someone had answered. He put the sixpence in and began talking. The very hunch of his back was a sneer to her.

"Selfish pig," she said. She went around to the other box in the wild hope that the post office had repaired it in the last hour, but the whole instrument had been pulled to bits by vandals. The smell that rushed out at her was enough to make her really sick. She let go of the door.

Her watch had stopped at twelve. She guessed the time to be about twenty to five and set the hands at that. She wound up the watch and then went to stand between the boxes and the wall in what she hoped was the most inconspicuous position. Why had she told Richard she was feeling ill? When she didn't come back after five minutes or so, he might start thinking she'd collapsed. He might go down and knock on the door.

She tried to work out how long she'd been out. It must have been more than five minutes. She was getting cold without a coat. She couldn't risk it much longer. As soon as that damned man put the phone down, she would go in there and physically haul him out.

The man was still talking. She looked at her watch. Quarter to five. Growing desperate, she walked to the door and started to pull it open.

"Excuse me—"

He thrust out at the door with his foot in a sudden movement, knocking her off balance. She lost her hold on the door, and it swung slowly shut. Furious now, she grabbed it again and pulled it open, holding onto the handle.

"I've an emergency call," she said. "How long are you going to be?"

He jerked his shoulder. "Use the phone next door."

"It's not working. Will you let me make this one call? Please!"

He half turned. "Listen, dear," he said, "you've got your troubles, I've got mine. All right?"

He put his hand around the edge of the door and pulled it shut. He gave her a nasty little grin. He wasn't going to budge. She couldn't believe anyone could behave like that. She was near tears from frustration and anger. She couldn't wait any longer. She'd have to go back to the house.

She almost ran back down the street. Mr. Morfitt was standing looking out of the shop window as she passed. He waved cheerily to her. She could tell he was going to come into the hall to talk to her. She rushed into the house and up the stairs before he could intercept her.

She stopped outside the flat to catch her breath. She gripped her hands together in a silent prayer. She got out her key and unlocked the door.

Richard was not in the kitchen. He called out to her from the living room. "I'm in here, Julie."

She went in. He was sitting on the sofa, arms spread out on either side of him along the back. He looked very relaxed.

"You were a long time," he said. "Are you all right?"

"Yes," she said. "Yes, I feel a little better."

The tray of tea was on the table in front of him. She sat down in the armchair and bent forward to pour out a cup of tea. It came out thick and orange.

"It's gone rather stale," he said. "Waiting for you."

"That's all right," she said. "I don't really want anything."

"Don't you?" He leaned forward suddenly and gripped her wrist. "I should have thought after all that rushing up and down, a nice cup of tea would have been just the thing to revive you."

She tensed, like a cat unwillingly held.

"You're cold," he said. "You shouldn't go running about the streets without a coat." He smiled. "You'll catch your death."

So he knew. Somehow he knew. Who had seen her? Robinson? She said nothing. He jerked her wrist, pulling her toward him until his face was only an inch away from hers.

"It's the wrong face, isn't it?" he said softly. "To quote an old English proverb: 'My face doesn't fit.'"

She found her voice. "No, it doesn't. You're not Richard."

"Ah—" He nodded. "That's what I wanted to know."

He let her go. She fell back into the armchair. She sat rubbing her wrist.

"There could be only one reason why you went off secretly to telephone, but I had to know for certain. I had to hear you say it."

He called out, and a man came in from the bedroom. The name he called was not Robinson, but then it had been obvious that would not be his real name. She had always thought Robinson was an unlikely name for the man who stood in the doorway.

She had seen from the beginning only glimpses of him. Now the snake had come slithering from the shadows.

It was strange how accurately she had been able to draw him, how the pale pitted face had marked her mind. Perhaps the professional killer carried an aura around with him that impressed itself on the most casual encounter.

Yet he passed about the city, unremarked and unquestioned. The respectable businessman of Morfitt's description, the clerk of Anne's, the petty thief of the agency girls'.

The atmosphere of the room had changed with his entrance. *He has cold eyes,* she thought, *very like a snake's. Expressionless.*

"I believe you've nearly met this gentleman before," Richard said.

"Mr. Robinson," Julie said. She put her opinion of him into the phrasing of his name.

Richard laughed. "She doesn't approve of you. What did you find?"

Julie saw then that Robinson had her handbag clutched in one hand. She turned to Richard. She spoke in a tense, abrupt tone.

"What was he doing in my bedroom? What is he doing with my handbag? Give it to me."

She wouldn't speak or look at Robinson. She wasn't afraid of him or of the man who controlled him. Now that the moment had come, she found she was past fear. She felt cold: not mentally cool and rational and clearheaded but physically cold. Her skin was icy.

Richard nodded. Robinson threw the bag to him. Richard caught it in one hand nonchalantly, like a cricketer fielding a toss. He handed it to Julie. She took it and put it carefully on the table by the window as if to let the circulating air decontaminate it.

"There was nothing in the bag or the bedroom," Robinson said. "Except the newspapers."

He had a light, pleasant voice. It seemed incongruous.

"Ah, yes, the newspapers," Richard said. He handed one folded to an inside page to Julie. "You saw this, of course. This is what made you suspect me." It was the story about Brochet.

She thought very quickly. Neither she nor Stephen, as far

as she knew, had mentioned to Richard anything about the body in the harbor. He must think the item in the paper was the first she had heard of it. It was the timing of the murder that would be so significant to Stephen if he happened to see that report. She had to cover up their knowledge of that timing.

"When I read that I wondered if it was an accident," she said. "He was involved, obviously, since he shot at you, but I've no idea who he was. He can't have been one of our security people. They wouldn't try to kill you. They'd sit and wait for you."

He nodded. "That is reasonable. But I couldn't be sure. I dealt with him before I met you at nine. I killed him because I could take no chances. Neither with him nor with Michael Brent. Any more than I can with you. What made you doubt me?"

"A lot of small things," she said, "in the way you talk."

"Ah—the way one talks, that is unimportant. That can be watched and improved."

"No, it can't," she said. "I've warned them. They are on their way. Whatever happens you're finished. I've told them you're not Richard."

"How?" he asked. "On the telephone?"

"Yes, just now. When I went out."

He shook his head. "Poor little Julie. That was our man in the telephone box. He got quite a shock when you stopped outside it. His duty was to follow you. He only went in there for cover to see which way you went when you got to the end of the street. Sensibly, he rang me here. I told him to stay put and on no account let you use the phone. So we know you told no one. It's no use pretending."

"I thought he was an unpleasant creature," she said. "I should have guessed he was a friend of yours."

"Yes, well—" He smiled. "One cannot expect to be liked."

He looked at Robinson. "Get going. I'll give you ten minutes."

He nodded. He left the flat without one glance at Julie.

"Where's he going?" She was suddenly terrified for Stephen. Then she remembered that as long as Richard remained uncertain about him, he was safe. While there was a possibility that Stephen was at this moment persuading Holbrook that every word of her letter was true, Richard would do nothing. With so much at stake he had to take every chance.

"Things could become rather difficult for Robinson after

your discoveries about Michael Brent," Richard was saying. "He's clearing out."

"What did he have in the cellar?"

"What you imagined. Equipment to tap your phone, wire this room, a radio for communications with our superiors. They had to know exactly how it was going before they could let me send that last postcard." He smiled. "Robinson said the place was a nest of nosy women. When we were sure you'd taken the bait, he got out. He said the house was like Piccadilly Circus as far as a quiet bit for breaking and entering was concerned."

"He doesn't look as if he's got much of a sense of humor."

"Well, that's freely translated. His version was a trifle simpler."

"He may be good at murder," she said, "but I wouldn't say he was much of a burglar. He made a lot of noise."

"Are you trying to give him a bad report?"

"Yes," she said. "I am. I hope he gets into trouble."

"You are a vindictive girl, aren't you?"

"What are you going to do with me?"

"Don't ask that, Julie," he said. "Don't think about it."

"Are you going to kill me here?"

"No." He looked at his watch.

"Stephen will be back soon. He's been gone an hour."

"He was meeting Holbrook half an hour after he left here, and he left at quarter to four. It's now ten to five. He's got to convince Holbrook I'm Richard Davidge, and once he's done that, they've got to decide what they're going to do about it. They won't rush anything. Don't forget they think we're threatened in here. They'll be very careful they don't trigger off a panic move by our 'enemies.' While the house is busy, they'll consider us safe. No, Julie, they won't be here for quite a while yet."

"So you don't think Stephen suspects you?"

"Not now. I realized that was an oversensitive reaction on my part. Think about it yourself. It's quite easy to prove. If Archer for one moment suspected me of being a double agent, he would never have left you with me. He would have sent you with the letter and stayed here himself."

It was true, obviously true. So she was the last one left. Though there was Dorothy.

"What are you going to do about Richard's wife?" she said. "Are you going to stage an accident for her, too?"

He shrugged. "It doesn't look as if it will be necessary

to do anything. I shall refuse to see her. I shall give her the divorce she wants. She'll be perfectly satisfied with that. She will congratulate herself on her acumen in detecting the difference between the man exchanged and her true husband."

"For someone who's never met her, you know her very well."

"I know you all very well."

"Except Michael Brent."

He frowned. "Yes. We hadn't taken him enough into consideration. He wasn't your lover, and he hadn't seen your brother for some years. We had him classed with acquaintances of Richard Davidge, not close friends. We never expected him to take action. That's why my reaction was blunt, to say the least. I couldn't take a risk on a man we had not sufficiently investigated."

"So your plan wasn't all that thorough." She was trying to keep him talking. Every minute she kept him talking was vital.

"On the contrary, it was exceedingly thorough," he replied. "You don't imagine this was something done on the spur of the moment. Of course, the exchange was rushed through, but that was merely to raise the first suspicions in the minds of Davidge's superiors. No, it was the death of his immediate superior that gave us the idea."

"Welford, you mean?"

"Yes. Welford had picked your brother, trained him, controlled him. He had kept him to himself. He briefed him and received his reports. He was the only man who could not be deceived. An interrogation by him would have destroyed any double agent impersonating Davidge, no matter how physically similar or perfectly briefed. They would have had certain things in common we could never have known about. When we received the report of his fatal heart attack, the possibility of substitution occurred for the first time."

He smiled at her in a friendly way. He was enjoying himself, she realized. It was the first moment of relaxation for him since the deception had begun, and as far as he could see, it was going to be the last. Once accepted as Richard Davidge, he would never be able to talk freely again.

"Your brother was, as far as we were concerned, ideally placed in his private life. No agent has a private life—his private life is his work—but most of them do have relatives and wives. In your brother's case, his wife was a stupid woman from whom he was separated and from whom we could foresee little trouble. His parents were dead. He had no children and no close friends, and his only living relative, his young sister, was ten years younger than he and had never been very close to him. On the other hand, she was bright and intelligent and her word would be accepted. She could be used."

"Used, and then disposed of, in case one of those child-hood memories you knew nothing about came to the surface?"

He did not reply.

"What about Stephen?" she asked.

"We had to give you someone to help you, to keep you away from the police. Archer had met your brother twice only but, considering that Davidge disappeared from Lyons, in circumstances that would make him remember him. He was a capable, experienced man who liked working on his own. We had to watch him, of course. He was our main risk. He was more experienced than you, Julie. He would not be as anxious as you were to rescue a brother in trouble. Once you left for France, we were pretty certain of the out-come, but he has been difficult to convince."

"So have I," she pointed out.

"Yes, I'm sorry about that." He even sounded sorry.

"You're taking me out of the house?"

He glanced at his watch again. "In another couple of minutes, yes."

"What if I won't go?"

He shook his head sadly. He produced a gun from his pocket and sat with it cradled in his hand. She had never seen an automatic at close quarters before. She did not really believe that any of this was happening to her. She was acting a part. If she stopped acting, she would start screaming. If he had known it, his matter-of-factness, his friendliness, his slight humor, was helping her. Perhaps he did know it. He wouldn't want a hysterical screaming female on his hands, would he? Would he?

"You're not going to shoot me here?" she said.

"Don't be such an idiot," he said mildly. "Of course not. Now don't make me use it, Julie."

"I wouldn't dream of encouraging you to use it." She gave a nervous smile. "While there's life, there's hope, they say."

"That's the way to look at it." He looked at his watch.

He didn't have a silencer on the gun. If he'd had a silencer, he could have shot her, and no one would have known. He could have spun some story about her saving his life from an intruder. Perhaps there hadn't been time for Robinson to bring him a silencer. It must have been Robinson who got him the gun.

"What are you going to tell Stephen?" she said.

"That you had told me you were going downstairs to the lavatory. That after five minutes or so, I discovered you had actually left the house. That you must have seen Robinson and gone after him. That you were so upset by Michael's death you would have gone rushing after his murderer without thinking of the danger. I would have rushed after you and been searching for you. We will then," he added precisely, "all start searching for you."

"Yes," she said. "He'd believe that. That's clever."

He inclined his head in acknowledgment.

"But why have you had to be so clever?" she asked. "Why all this elaborate charade? Why not just exchange the wrong man for Richard in a simple, straightforward way? You'd achieve the same thing with less trouble."

He shook his head. "A man exchanged is an object of careful scrutiny, even suspicion, at least at first. He is not likely to be used in any confidential position until they are absolutely certain of him. He is closely interrogated and watched. The odds against getting a double agent accepted that way are too great. And substitution is a possibility that might just occur to the security boys. They are a suspicious lot.

"A man who escapes, however, who makes his way home, who reveals to them a devastatingly brilliant deception that had taken them all in, such a man is welcomed with open arms, praised, promoted—and not questioned nearly so closely, not at least in the first furor of discovery. Such a man would be readily accepted, particularly when helped and sworn to by his only living relative. The authorities would be only too pleased to have been rescued from a monumental mistake."

"Psychology," she said.

"Yes. The psychology of the feint in fencing and boxing and so many other sports. The double bluff."

There was a silence. He glanced at the phone. She was beginning to get frightened. It was like coming out of anesthesia into a consciousness of reality. She didn't dare look at her own situation. She didn't dare face it. It would paralyze her.

She said, "You've got a man outside, haven't you? The man in the phone box. What's he doing?"

"Keeping an eye open for any sudden activity. He'll ring me if anything happens. Give me warning." He looked at his watch. "Ten minutes are up. Time to go." He gave her quite an affectionate smile. "They're not coming yet, you see. I don't suppose they'll be here for quite half an hour. And they daren't telephone. I'm sorry, Julie, but there it is. The luck of the game."

"Stephen commented on the way you patronize me," she said. "He didn't like it and neither do I."

He seemed amused. "Very well, I apologize. I don't mean to sound patronizing."

The typewriters upstairs had stopped. She could imagine Miss Dawson and Denise and the other girl whose name she could never remember, gathering up the last of the day's work and sorting out the post and putting the kettle on for the last cup of instant coffee. Downstairs Mr. Morfitt would be having a cup of tea in the back room before the final half hour's trading of the day, the five thirty custom of the people who bought things on their way home from the office and who were the only reason he kept open till six. A quiet, peaceful moment of the day in this house.

Richard stood up. He had put the gun back in his pocket. He didn't think he was going to need it. He was still, in his way, patronizing her.

"Time to go," he repeated. "Come on."

"I want a coat," she said.

"I saw a raincoat hanging in the hall. We'll pick it up as we go out."

She stood up, too. He backed away toward the door. He was being, from habit, quite careful.

"Once we get downstairs," he said quietly, "I'll shoot you, you know, if you run."

"I shan't run."

She looked around. "Where's my handbag?"

He was getting impatient. "You don't need—"

"I would never go anywhere without my handbag. It's instinctive."

He said sharply, "It's over there. On the table."

She had known very well where it was. She hadn't wanted

him to have any doubts about what she was doing when she moved. The handbag was where she had put it, on the table by the window. The table where the telephone stood.

He opened the door into the hall. The inner doors of the flat fitted quite well. They had been put in at the time of the conversion and were reasonably new. The front door of the flat was the original. It had warped over the years, helped by the wartime blasts of nearby bombs which had shaken the whole street to its foundations more than once. There was quite a large gap between the bottom of the door and the floor. In winter it got very drafty in the flat if you didn't close the inside doors. Sound carried through that door.

He was in the hall. He was taking the raincoat off a hook. He was still watching her. She moved across to the table. She picked up handbag and telephone in one movement and flung them with all her strength at the window. The telephone crashed through the glass into the street. It made a shattering explosive noise. As she threw it, she began screaming. She screamed at the top of her voice. She saw the gun in his hand. She dropped behind the sofa as he fired the first shot.

She heard the second shot. She was deafened and hysterical. Screaming made her feel hysterical. She never screamed. There was broken glass behind the sofa. She didn't dare move. She didn't know what he was doing. Any moment she would look up and see him above her, staring down at her as he shot her. She heard noises from above, thumps and running feet. No, the feet weren't up above. They were on the stairs. There was someone shouting from below, and then Miss Dawson's voice calling her name. *Oh, God,* she thought, *I hope he doesn't shoot Miss Dawson.* She stopped screaming.

A door slammed. Her door. He had run for it. He'd gone. She lay there amid the glass, too weak to move. She couldn't believe she'd done it, that he'd gone. She felt too limp to call out. She would wait here till they found her. Till she heard a voice she knew speak her name. And then suddenly she knew she was wrong. He hadn't gone. She could feel his presence in the room. He must have banged the door to make her think he'd gone. To make her get up. When she stood up, he'd be there waiting, and he'd kill her.

He wasn't waiting. He was coming across the room. She could feel through the floorboards the faint vibration of his tread. In a moment, he would be here. What had happened to the others? Oh, Lord, they'd all rushed down to the street. They'd gone to see what had been thrown out. She should have thought of that. By the time they came to the flat it would be too late. It was too late. He was here.

He put a knee on the sofa and leaned over it. She looked up into his face. It was Stephen.

"Well," he said, "you certainly wrecked that phone, didn't you?"

Julie Davidge and her burglars were going to be a nine days' wonder. Everyone in the house commented on her presence of mind. Upstairs in the agency they'd heard the noise and the screaming and had rushed down to help. As Miss Dawson and the girls reached the flat, that young man who'd been staying with her, her relative, had come running out. "Downstairs!" he'd cried and leaped down the stairs to the street with them all close behind him. Mr. Morfitt was outside on the pavement, and his customers. There seemed to be a lot of customers. When one of them had drawn a revolver, Miss Dawson had tried to take it from him. She had actually tried to kick it out of his hand, and it had taken two men to hold her. How was she to know they were all policemen? They said they were very impressed with her strength. Denise had even had to vouch for her. They had suspected her because of her efforts to get the gun. She had created quite a diversion, they told her. Miss Davidge's relative had slipped away during their struggle with her. They appeared to be quite worried about that. She supposed they were afraid he might get hurt, chasing the crooks.

It was Mr. Robinson, of course. She'd seen him hunched up in a police car, handcuffed to a policeman. And another man with him, too. It was only after that she'd remembered she hadn't seen Julie. "But when we got upstairs, you were all right, weren't you, thank heaven, dear, and with that nice-looking young man looking after you. Not at all, don't thank me. It was most exciting. It's made me feel quite part of the London scene."

"So he got away." They were sitting in the living room of her brother's flat in Regent's Park, Stephen and David Holbrook and Julie and Richard, the real Richard.

"Don't worry, Miss Davidge," Holbrook said. "We'll pick him up. We've got a net out for him. The police are in on it with us."

"He'll make for the embassy," Richard said. "They'll ship him out as a returning chauffeur or sick crook or whatever when the heat's died down."

"Isn't that undiplomatic?" Julie said. "I thought that sort of thing wasn't allowed."

"It's an undiplomatic business," Holbrook said.

"He decided you couldn't suspect him," she told Stephen "because if you had, you would never have left me to his tender mercies."

"I didn't think he'd harm you," Stephen said. "I thought you were essential to him. It never occurred to me you'd have some blinding flash of intuition while I was away."

"It wasn't intuition," she said. "It was tomatoes."

"Tomatoes?"

Richard laughed. "I never thought of that." He explained to the others. "I'm allergic to tomatoes. Always have been. They make me ill."

"I never knew that," Holbrook said.

"It never arose. The last time I ate them was when I was about seven."

Julie said to Stephen, "And it would have been helpful if you'd told me what you were up to. I thought you accepted him, like me."

"I did and I didn't," he said. "I've spent most of the time in a state of utter confusion. For example. I didn't recognize the man in St.-Malo at all. He seemed the right height and the right coloring, but apart from that it could have been anybody. But I'd only seen him twice before, after all, and at that point I couldn't think who the hell it could be if not your brother. I mean what else could the postcards and so on and those fellows in the green car tailing us mean but that? And you seemed to know him, Julie. So I went along with it. But the funny thing was, I didn't like him. Now when I met Richard here in Lyons, I liked him at once. We got on together. We were on the same wavelength. That's something that doesn't change. I suppose I smelled him out, like a dog. Then there was the business of Brochet. If anything happened to Brochet, I told myself, I would know what it meant. I was convinced he was a perfectly harmless character who liked a pretty face. I couldn't believe it when Richard said he'd fired a gun at him, but I thought he was simply mistaken about the source of the shot. It never occurred to me that there had been no shot, or that Brochet was dead. Until we got to Jersey and heard about the body in the harbor. I was thinking about that when Richard swam ashore. Very power-ful swimmer, very good well-developed physique for a man who'd been two and a half years in prison. But I couldn't tell you any of this, Julie. The more convinced you were by him, the safer for you, at that stage. Then we got back and found out about Michael's murder. That confused me again. That looked like proof we had brought back the real Davidge, after all. And then it occurred to me it could work both ways. His death could mean he had discovered the exchanged Davidge was the real one. It could mean they were afraid he might know incidents the phony one was unaware of, so they couldn't be allowed to meet."

"The ironic thing is," Richard said, "he never came to see me."

"He wouldn't without ringing me first," Julie said. "I can see that now. He'd check with me first. That was why he was telephoning me. To see if it would be all right for him to visit Richard. Nothing else."

"And then there was the letter," Stephen said. "He was so insistent that Julie was to write it. Why couldn't he have written, too? Why wouldn't he ring up and talk to you, Hol-brook, or one of his old friends in the department? It wouldn't have mattered if the phone had been tapped. The message would have got through, and after that, it would be pointless to try to kill him since the plot would already have been blown sky high. No, he kept talking about speed, but he wouldn't take the obvious and fastest action. I decided if Julie set off with that letter, she wouldn't get there. She'd be found dead, on Holbrook's doorstep probably, with the letter clutched significantly in her hand. So I decided to take it myself. And when I reached Holbrook, Julie, I found him on my side."

"He means equally confused," Holbrook said. "Though we were curious. We thought there was something a bit odd about that exchange. We thought something funny was happening. We kept a watch on you and your flat on and off. We found out you'd gone to France. We picked you up and followed you to Caen and then lost you. That made us even more suspicious. We waited for you to come back. Our man reported someone else was watching the house, too. That was further confusion. Then Archer rang me up and said he had to see me urgently about your brother. When he arrived, we compared notes and still weren't sure of the answer. We decided to move in and wait for something to happen. We picked up one suspect, the man who had been watching the house."

"The man who prevented me from ringing you," Julie said.

"Yes. We got him and then we got Robinson. He came out of the house as we arrived. We were just deciding to come in and fetch you when the phone came out of the window."

"So you weren't sure, until then?"

"No, we weren't sure. But even if he'd killed you, Miss Davidge, and we'd been left with your letter and two men both claiming to be your brother, he wouldn't have won. We'd have accepted neither, rather than take the wrong one."

"Then he would have won," Stephen said. "He'd have made Richard useless. Whereas now—"

"Yes," Holbrook admitted. "In that sense he would have won."

"Richard," Julie said. "I'm sorry. I'm sorry I ever doubted you." She took his hand. "They were too clever for me with their rotten postcards."

"I would have known another Julie as a fake any day of the year," he said. "But then I'm not quite so remarkable."

"Her face is more difficult to copy, too," Stephen said.

Richard laughed. "Well, there is that." He touched her gently on the chin. "If I'd realized how important you were going to be to me, I'd have paid you more attention."

"You remember my second visit," she said. "I kept trying to trick you with questions."

"Yes, I thought so. I thought Holbrook had put you up to it. I was very angry. I wouldn't play."

"You could have solved everything at one swoop if you had. When I asked you about that summer on the Wye, for instance. He wouldn't have known about that walk we took."

He shook his head. "It wouldn't have helped. I don't remember anything about any walks. The only thing I remember about that summer is the flies."

Holbrook left them at seven, "to do a little work," as he put it, but by an inspired flight of fancy he had a four-course meal sent in with a couple of bottles of champagne. It was a gesture, Richard remarked, that would do for the time being. When he considered how much they owed Julie, he'd no doubt be around with the odd few diamonds.

"I'm the one who'll be giving her diamonds," Stephen said. "Holbrook can keep his distance."

"Good God," Richard said. "Really? Congratulations."

"I'm getting a special license tomorrow. She gets in too much trouble on her own." He put his arm around Julie. "I did ask you to marry me, didn't I?"

"I believe so," she said. "I can't quite remember. It's been such a long courtship."

"We'll let you know the details, Richard," Stephen said. "Will you come?"

"Come? I'll give her away."

"I suppose I'll have to give up the flat," Julie said. "I was happy there for a long time. But it's changed now."

"Everything changes," Richard said.

She smiled at him. "That's the sort of deep philosophy one expects from elder brothers."

He grinned, and reached one casual hand down the side of his armchair to the bottle standing on the carpet. "Let's finish the champagne."

"We might keep the flat on," Stephen said, "for a year or so. It would save hotel bills. And you could stay there when I'm abroad, and get on with artistic bits of work to swell the coffers. Richard could keep an eye on you."

"More likely the other way round. And I shall get on with my artistic little works wherever we are—" She broke off. "Oh, dear, I wish Mike wasn't dead."

Stephen put his hand over hers. "I'm sorry. I should learn to keep my mouth shut."

"I don't know why it is," Richard said. "It's always the nice people who seem to get hurt."

"That's funny," Julie said. "That's exactly what he said. Your substitute. He sounded almost as if he meant it, at the time."

Stephen pulled himself to his feet. "I ought to be going. Let you rest. It's getting quite late."

Julie was staying in Richard's flat that night. Holbrook, apparently, hadn't thought it very wise for her to remain in her own place.

Stephen kissed her. "Good night, love." He called back to Richard. "I'll look in at the flat below on my way out. See if there's any news."

There couldn't have been any news because he didn't come back.

Julie went to bed. It was an unfamiliar room and bed. She had never slept overnight in this flat. She did not expect to sleep, but she went out like Richard's felled oak. She dreamed about him. In her dream everything was mixed up;

Brochet and her brother and the false Richard and the sea and bells ringing and Miss Dawson and the phone smashing through the window. In her dream it hung there, swinging from its cord out of the window and ringing and ringing. . . .

She was wide awake. She was in her brother's flat in the dark, and the phone was ringing.

She felt for her dressing gown and pulled it on. She opened the door and went on bare feet into the living room. The phone had stopped. Richard had answered it. He was standing there, in a red dressing gown, listening to someone speaking fast at the other end.

"Right," he said. "Thank you. Thanks for letting me know."

He put the phone down. Turning, he saw Julie.

"What is it?" she said.

"It's nothing. I'm sorry you were awakened. You'd better go back to bed."

"Richard," she said quietly. "What was that phone call about?"

He put his hands in his pockets in a resigned gesture. "Well, it doesn't really matter your knowing. It doesn't mean anything. That was Holbrook. They've been questioning those two men they picked up."

"You mean Robinson and the other man?"

"Yes. From what they say, they think the man who has been impersonating me may try to silence me. I suppose in the other side's view I could still be useful to my department, and they didn't send me over here in order to let me go on with my work. I was supposed to be discredited and possibly shot. Since he's failed one way, they think he may try another, more direct approach."

"Richard—"

He shrugged it off. "It's all melodrama. Nothing like that's going to happen. But Holbrook's phoning the flat downstairs to send one of their men up. He'd like one of them on duty inside this flat. Just to be on the safe side. We can go back to bed and sleep, and he can sit up with the mice. It's a waste of time, but there you are. You might as well go back to bed. I'm going to as soon as I've let him in."

He looked at his watch. "There are two men downstairs. One on duty and one asleep. The man on duty will have to stay by the phone, so he'll have to wake the other one, then the man will have to get dressed and get up here. He'll be about five or ten minutes, I should think. Since you are up, do you want a nightcap?"

The doorbell rang.

"That's quick. He can't have gone to bed. I'll let him in."

She sank down on the sofa, yawning, and tucked her feet under her to keep warm. She heard Richard open the front door and the low murmur of voices. Richard was wearing slippers. The other man's heels clicked on the tile floor of the hall. She heard Richard say, "We might as well have some whiskey while we're waiting." So he wasn't going back to bed. He was taking it seriously.

The two men came in. Julie half pulled herself upright, ready to be polite.

He had shaved off his beard. He had found himself a suit, and a pair of ordinary shoes. He had not put back the dark glasses. He looked as Richard had five years before. Very like, but not like enough. Not now. It was like seeing a photograph of someone and knowing it was him because you were there when the photograph was taken and yet not seeing him in the photograph, not recognizing the personality you knew, because the years and the experience of those years had altered that familiar face in so many subtle ways.

She said, "Richard!"

They both turned to her. Both. With a twin reaction. Then the false Richard had a gun in his hand, and this time it had a silencer. At the same instant, her brother shot him dead, firing through the pocket of his dressing gown.

The shot echoed, echoed around the room. There was an acrid smell. She stared at the crumpled body on the floor.

"I should have remembered," Richard said, "that the simplest way of getting in somewhere is to ring the bell."

The gun with its silencer lay near the limp right hand.

"Why did he wait?" she said. "Why didn't he shoot you in the hall?"

"I welcomed him in. I had my hand on his arm as we came in. It must have taken him aback. He had no opportunity."

She said, "I didn't know you had a gun."

"The remarkable thing is," he said, "I didn't recognize him. I didn't see myself in him."

"We none of us know what we really look like," Julie said. "That's what they say, isn't it? Mirrors are the wrong way around, and cameras are one-dimensional. They tell us something, but it's never the truth. Other people have to give us the truth."

The doorbell rang. Richard put his automatic down on the table and went to answer it. Julie sat down and rested her head in her hands. She was not, at that stage, surprised when a few minutes later Stephen came in and sat beside her and put an arm around her.

"I always come too late," he said.

She shook her head. "No, not too late." She looked at him. "How did you come to be here?"

Richard came back into the room. He was carrying a rug. He threw it over the body of the man whose name she had never known, and went to the telephone. He began dialing a number.

"I stayed in the flat below," Stephen said. "I didn't want to be too far from you. Holbrook telephoned. Here I am."

She held on to his hand. "Don't go away again."

"No," he said. "I won't."

It was very quiet in the room, very still. She leaned her cheek against his shoulder.

She heard Richard say on the phone, "It's all over. He's dead."

She closed her eyes.